The Wrong Brother

The Wrong Brother
Montana Made Romance

Eve Gaddy

The Wrong Brother
Copyright© 2024 Eve Gaddy
Tule Publishing First Printing August 2024

The Tule Publishing, Inc.

ALL RIGHTS RESERVED

First Publication by Tule Publishing 2024

Cover Design by Lee Hyatt Designs

No part of this book may be used or reproduced in any manner whatsoever without written permission except in the case of brief quotations embodied in critical articles and reviews.

This is a work of fiction. Names, characters, places, and incidents are products of the author's imagination or are used fictitiously. Any resemblance to actual events, locales, organizations, or persons, living or dead, is entirely coincidental.

AI was not used to create any part of this book and no part of this book may be used for generative training.

ISBN: 978-1-964703-19-0

Chapter One

Dr. Logan McFarland stared disbelievingly at his brother Liam. "You've invited a woman you've never even met in person to come stay with us? Why?"

Liam looked up from the saddle he was cleaning and frowned. "I'm thinking about getting married."

"To a woman you met over the internet? Are you nuts?"

"No." He gave Logan a speculative glance. "Did you know Clint asked Mom to marry him?"

Clint Westbrook owned one of the neighboring ranches. He'd lost his wife years ago and had been sweet on their mother for as long as she'd been a widow. Which was several years ago now.

"Good for him. It's about time. What does that have to do with anything?"

Liam shook his head. "It has everything to do with it. She said no."

"What? She's crazy about the man. Did she tell you why she turned him down? And why hasn't she said anything to me or Connor?"

"She didn't tell me either. I overheard her and Velma

having an argument."

Velma Fay was their housekeeper who'd been with them forever. "I know she and Velma are close but why the hell would she talk to Velma and not us?"

"She doesn't want us to know. Mom told Velma she wouldn't marry Clint because then she'd have to leave the ranch. And she won't leave the ranch until I'm settled," Liam said, making air quotes for the last word.

Logan stared at him. "That's ridiculous."

Liam stood and shrugged. "That's Mom. You know how stubborn she is when she makes up her mind."

"And she didn't tell you. Only Velma."

"Right. Because she doesn't want to force me into marrying someone. But she's worried I never will. On account of Caroline."

Caroline. The woman who'd left his brother at the altar to run off with another man. "You're not still hung up on her, are you?"

"Hell, no. But there's also no one around here who doesn't know that story."

"So?"

"So I want a fresh start. And Cici Bradley could be it. We've been corresponding for a couple of months now and she's coming here. Next week."

"Does she know you're thinking about marriage?" To some woman he'd never actually met. How crazy was that?

"She knows I want to settle down eventually. I think she

does too. But no, marriage hasn't come up. We haven't even met in person yet."

"You think she wants to settle down but you're not sure?" Liam rolled his eyes but didn't answer. "How long is she staying?"

"We left it open." He picked up the clean saddle and hung it up on the wall.

Logan shook his head, watching his brother pick up another saddle, put it on the block and start to clean it. "So she can just up and leave her job?"

"She's a writer. She says she can write from anywhere."

"What does she write? Is she published?"

"Fiction. And yes. I don't know that much about it. We'll talk more once she gets here."

"What if you're not attracted to each other? Have you thought of that?"

"Zoom, remember? We've seen each other plenty of times. She's gorgeous."

"Virtually. Not the same thing, bro. Besides, if she's so gorgeous why is she coming to Montana to possibly marry a guy she's never met in person? Where's she from anyway?"

"Texas."

"So this gorgeous woman can't find a guy in Texas? Sounds pretty fishy to me." Hell, he'd lived in Texas during medical school. You couldn't tell him she couldn't find a man in Texas.

"I'm not asking for your approval."

"Good, because you're not getting it."

"I thought about not telling you, but I didn't want you showing up here and being an ass when you met her. If you can't be decent to her then don't come around."

"How? I live here too."

"You're at the hospital as much as you are here."

An exaggeration but not by much. He was a surgeon and rather than drive back and forth between the ranch and the hospital he often chose to stay at the hospital when he was on call.

"Have you told Mom?"

"Of course. But as far as she's concerned this has nothing to do with her and Clint. Cici's staying with us, and I wanted to make sure she knew my mother lived here too. So she'd be more comfortable."

"Mom's okay with this?"

"I'm a grown-ass man. My mother doesn't run my life."

"You're a dumb-ass man. Mom might not run your life, but she'll figure out what you're doing and why. And then there'll be hell to pay."

"Not if we don't tell her. She knows I met Cici over the internet and we liked each other. And that she's coming here so we can get to know each other."

"I thought those online dating things put people who lived near each other together."

"Some do. Some don't if you request to meet people from farther away or even other states."

"She knows you're a rancher, right?"

"Duh. It's part of my profile. Besides, I've sent her pictures of the ranch and the town."

"Your profile? Like hardworking rancher needs female companionship?"

"Ha ha. There's a lot more to it."

"You've met other women through this thing?"

"Actually, no. She's the first."

"Oh, my God, Liam. This is a disaster waiting to happen."

"Why? The worst that happens is we figure out we're not suited to each other. In which case I'll try again."

Logan left the barn before he exploded, tracking his mother down to the kitchen where she was talking to Velma.

"Mom, can I talk to you?"

"Of course."

Velma undoubtedly knew about Cici. Even so, he wanted to talk to his mother alone. "Let's go in the den."

Velma snorted but didn't say anything. His mother followed him, looking puzzled. "What is it, honey?"

"Liam's lost his mind."

She laughed and took a seat on the couch. "You heard about Cici, I take it."

He paced a few steps. "Are you telling me you're okay with this craziness?"

"They met through a dating service. Lots of people use them. What harm could there be?"

"What's wrong with the women around here? Why can't he date one of them?"

"You know why. Caroline jilting him played hell with his ego. He's convinced every woman around here thinks he's a loser."

"Bullshit. More likely they think she was a bitch. Which she was." And a liar. A woman who wasn't at all who Liam had thought she was. Like Beth, who Logan had fallen for during his residency and who was the major reason he'd been content to play the field since then.

"I pointed that out. He said that was even worse. He says he doesn't need anyone's pity."

"So he wants to hook up with a woman he met over the internet?"

"Oh, for heaven's sake, Logan. They're not 'hooking up.' At least, I don't think they are. They haven't even met in person yet. Relax. It's all going to turn out fine."

And what happens if it doesn't?

CECELIA OWEN COULDN'T wait to get out of Texas. She was a born and raised Texan and two years ago she wouldn't have believed she'd be so anxious to leave her home state. Of course, two years ago she hadn't known her parents were felons. But she wasn't going to think about them and their Ponzi scheme. She was leaving Texas so she didn't have to be constantly reminded of a damned traumatic experience she never wanted to think about again. But that seemed impossible living in Fort Worth.

She'd decided to leave town because she could hardly show her face in her hometown. Everyone had heard about, or worse, been victimized by, the Ponzi scheme her parents had perpetrated. Most of them figured she'd been involved regardless of the fact that she'd turned them in and testified at the trial. God, she never wanted to go through something like that again. Thank God the national news outlets hadn't picked up the story. Everyone in her hometown, and probably the state, knowing was bad enough. She figured the only thing left for her was to get out of the state, for a while, anyway. Her best friend Roxanne had tried to convince her this would all blow over, but she wasn't going to hang around until it did. If it did.

On a whim, she'd signed up with Matchmakers.com, a dating service that specialized in connecting people with matching profiles, regardless of where they lived. You could specify where you didn't want to go, but otherwise you could get matched with anyone who was of similar interests, et cetera. She'd signed up under her pen name, Cici Bradley, and had requested someone in the US but beyond that she hadn't cared. And honestly, she held out very little hope that anything would come of this scheme. Wincing, she reminded herself it wasn't a scheme. That word held far too many negative connotations given what her parents had done.

She met a couple of men online, one who lived in Las Vegas and one who lived in Juneau. They were both nice and they video-chatted a few times, but there was no spark. Certainly not enough to warrant going to Nevada or Alaska to meet them in person. She was beginning to think that video-chatting wasn't a fair way to judge a man. Then she met Liam McFarland.

First, not to be shallow, but he was damn good-looking. Tall and lean, with brown hair, hazel eyes, and a decisive jaw, he made a woman look twice. He was a rancher, raising horses and cattle and he lived near a small town in Montana. They got along well, and they had some similar interests. Not a lot, but some, and she was sure they'd find more once they got to know each other better. She really enjoyed talking to him. The town he lived near was small and rural, which sounded and looked appealing, even though she was a city girl through and through. The past couple of years had soured her on city life. So when Liam suggested she come to Marietta and stay with him for a while and see how they felt meeting in person, she accepted. She'd been wary of staying with him, because after all, she didn't really know him, but when he told her his mother and brother lived on the ranch as well, she decided to accept his invitation.

So here she was on a plane flying to Bozeman, Montana, the city nearest Marietta with an airport. They'd argued over who was going to pay for the airline ticket, but Liam insisted and she discovered that once he made up his mind there was no changing it. Liam said he'd pick her up.

What's the worst that can happen? We decide this is never going to work and I go home. Or maybe I won't. Maybe I'll like it and I'll stay in small-town Montana. Maybe it will inspire my writing, which I've been having a hard time with since the shit hit the fan with my parents. Or maybe Liam and I will fall madly in love with each other and live happily ever after.

Nah. I couldn't be that lucky.

Chapter Two

"You need me to what?" Logan asked his brother. He'd known something was up when one of the hands came up to the house to get him, rather than Liam calling him from the barn.

"I need you to go to the Bozeman airport and pick up Cici. Her plane gets in this afternoon."

He started to ask Liam why the hell he couldn't do it himself, but since Liam was sitting in the birthing stall with his prize mare about to foal, he knew the answer. "How did you know I wasn't working?"

"You told me yesterday that you'd be here."

Oh, yeah. "Why can't Wendall do it?" Wendall was one of the hands—actually, the only full-time person Liam had. He had a few part-timers, but none of them were very dependable.

"I had to fire him."

"Why?" Logan couldn't figure out why it was so hard for Liam to find more help. Sometimes he thought his brother just didn't want to badly enough.

"He showed up drunk. Twice. So I fired him."

"Drunk? At six thirty in the morning?"

"Yeah. Twice. Gave me some sob story about a woman, but it was bullshit." He shook his head. "I rest my case."

"What about one of the others?"

Liam shrugged. "It's bad enough I'm not going to get her. Better my brother than someone who works for me."

"Connor might—"

"Nope. He's working."

Typical. Logan wished he was at work. "What about Mom?"

"She went to town. It's her poker day."

"Oh, yeah." His mom's group of friends got together every week to play poker. No bridge for them. "Does she know Moondance is in labor?" Their mother was a horsewoman and wouldn't miss the birth of a foal if she could help it.

"She's on her way home. But she wants to help me with the mare. Not drive to the airport."

That was no surprise. "What if I'd been working?"

Liam took his eyes off the mare to look at him. "You're not."

Crap. Nothing else to say but yes. He sighed heavily. "When does her plane get in?"

Liam told him, adding, "If you leave now you should make it in time. And be nice."

So that's how he made it to the airport with no time to spare. Except her plane was late so it hadn't mattered. He figured he'd recognize the woman. Liam had shown him her picture on his computer. She was pretty, he'd give him that. But he wouldn't call her gorgeous. Still, he couldn't figure out why she couldn't find someone to date in Texas. Fishy. Very fishy.

And as for Liam, Logan knew damn good and well his brother could have had his pick of women in Marietta or nearby. Liam ran a successful ranch, was generally a nice guy, and Logan had heard more than one woman gush about his looks. But Caroline's betrayal had ruined local women for Liam. So Liam had tried online dating. With women in other states yet.

Finally, the plane landed, and he watched the people moving past him. Then he saw her. Long, dark hair streaming over her shoulders and down her back. Absolutely perfect features. Big brown eyes, high cheekbones, a mouth made for kissing and a figure that even in jeans and a button-down shirt made a man itch to put his hands on her. Holy shit, Liam had been right. The woman was gorgeous.

Realizing she'd walked right past him while he stared, he hurried to catch up. "Cici?"

She turned around and looked at him, her expression slightly puzzled. "Yes?"

"I'm Logan McFarland. Liam's brother."

"Oh, I didn't see you. You do look a lot like Liam. Wasn't he supposed to pick me up?"

"Yes, but he had an emergency and asked me to do it."

"I see." She didn't appear convinced of the emergency.

"The baggage claim is this way."

"This is all I brought," she said, indicating her rolling carry-on and the backpack perched on top of it.

She must not be planning to stay long. "Can I take your bags for you?"

"Thanks, but I've got them."

Before long they were in his truck and headed to the ranch. She appeared to be perfectly content with silence. Oddly, since he disliked women who chattered, he felt uncomfortable with it. "Liam's prize mare is foaling. That's why he couldn't come. You know he raises quarter horses, don't you?"

"Yes, he told me. Is he worried about the horse?"

"Not exactly. But this is her first foal, and he wants to be on hand in case something goes wrong."

"Does that happen often? Something going wrong, I mean."

"I wouldn't say often, but it happens." He glanced at her. "So you're from Texas. Where in Texas?"

"The DFW metroplex."

Well, that was vague. "Which part? I went to medical school in Dallas."

"Fort Worth."

"I've been to Fort Worth a time or two. Nice town."

She didn't answer that, so he tried again. "Liam said you were a published author and you write fiction. What kind of fiction?" he asked, making a bet with himself that she'd say romance.

"I write thrillers."

"Really? I read thrillers sometimes. Would I have heard of you? Do you write as Cici Bradley?"

"I have no idea if you would have heard of any of my books. Look me up on the internet. And yes, Cici Bradley."

"I will."

They lapsed into silence, but Cici broke it after a little while. "So you're the doctor."

"I'm a surgeon. Our brother Connor is a paramedic."

"But Liam had no interest in medicine?"

Logan laughed. "Liam's a lot more interested in horses than in medicine. Unless it's horse medicine. What about you? How do you feel about horses?"

"They're pretty."

"And?"

"Very pretty?"

"I take it you don't know much about them. Or about ranch life."

"Not really. I rode some when I was younger. But it's been so long I don't remember much about it. Liam sent pictures though. It looks like a pretty place."

They turned off the highway onto the road that led to the ranch. Logan got out and opened the gate, got back in and drove over the cattle guard, then got back out to close the gate.

"You have to do that every time you come or go from the ranch?"

"Yeah. Why?"

"Seems like a pain."

Logan shrugged. "Just part of living on a ranch." As they neared the house, he decided this might be not just the best but his only chance to find out what she was really doing here. "Why did you leave Texas to come to the middle of Nowhere, Montana, to see a man you've never even met in person?"

CAUGHT TOTALLY OFF-GUARD, Cici stared at Logan. He'd gone from being nice enough, though not extremely welcoming, to suspicious and abrupt in the blink of an eye. "Excuse me?"

"I'm wondering what you're doing here."

"You know what I'm doing here. Meeting your brother in person."

"Yes, but why? What's wrong with Texas men?"

Hello. WTH? "Where is this coming from?"

"It seems odd to me that you'd come all the way from Texas to meet in person some guy you found on the internet."

Now he was pissing her off. "How is this your business? And how do you know Liam and I haven't already discussed my reasons?"

"Have you?"

"That's none of your business."

"So you haven't. Which means you're either running from something or hiding from something. Or someone."

Of course, she was running from something. She'd bet most of the people who wanted the hell out of where they lived were running from something. Her problem just happened to be her parents. The felons.

Of course, that wasn't the only reason she was here. But Dr. Nosy McFarland didn't need to know her reasons.

Fortunately they reached the farmhouse. It was a large, pretty, two-story house with white wood siding and a green shingled roof. A wide wraparound porch with wooden posts every few feet was filled with hanging plants and pots of flowers. Two wooden rockers and a porch swing completed the cozy picture.

Instead of responding she got out of the truck and slammed the door, jerking open the back door to grab her things out of the extended cab. "Thanks for the ride," she said and slammed that door too.

Logan got out and called, "Want me to help with your bags?"

She shot him the bird and kept walking. His laughter followed her.

A woman in her early fifties stepped out on the front porch to greet her. "You must be Cici. I'm Velma, the housekeeper. Let me take your bag."

"Thank you," she said rather than argue. Cici glanced at Logan ambling to the porch with a satisfied smile on his face. She wanted to punch him. How dare he lull her into thinking he was a nice guy only to turn into an ass?

"Logan, what's the matter with you? Get over here and carry these bags up to the blue room." To Cici she said, "Liam's still with his mare and so is his mother. Logan can take you down there once you're settled."

"Just point me to it. I'm sure I can find the way."

"Nonsense. Logan doesn't mind."

Logan had grabbed her bags and gone inside. She followed Velma inside, glancing around at the living room, a comfortable room with leather furniture, a couple of overstuffed chairs, a TV hanging on the wall across from the couch, and a stone fireplace. The room was light and airy, with large windows opening to a magnificent vista of mountains in the distance. "Oh, how beautiful."

"It's a nice view," Velma agreed. "I'll show you to your room so you can freshen up and then I'm sure you'll want to see Liam. Would you like something to eat or drink first?"

"No, I'm good, thanks."

They passed Logan on the stairs, heading down as they went up. Neither spoke. "I don't know what's gotten into that boy," Velma said. "Was he rude to you?"

It would serve him right if she said yes. She imagined Velma would take him to task. But she didn't believe in whining—well, not much. "No, not at all."

She wondered why Logan had such a bug up his nose about her. Was there a reason he didn't trust his brother to know his own business best? Or was he simply being a concerned brother?

Chapter Three

LOGAN TOOK HER down to the barn. "Velma didn't lecture me. Why didn't you rat me out?"

She stuck her nose in the air. "I don't know what you mean."

"Yes, you do."

"Oh, you mean the obnoxious interrogation you treated me to?"

He smiled. "Yeah, that."

Too bad his smile made him even more handsome. If Liam was good-looking, Logan was dreamy. His dark brown hair was a shade or two darker than Liam's but cut shorter. He had strong features and gray eyes that were sharp and intelligent. "I didn't see the point in it. And even though it's absolutely none of your business I cut you a break because I can see you're concerned for your brother." She paused and added, "But he's a grown man and I imagine he knows what he's doing."

Logan didn't say anything but his expression said it all. Well, he'd just have to get over it. She wasn't about to give up yet. She'd only just arrived, after all. She hadn't even seen

Liam yet.

The barn was open. Stepping inside to the central aisle Logan called out, "Liam, she's here."

"Be there in a minute."

She looked around, interested to see a number of horse stalls, most of which were empty. "Where are all the horses?"

"In the pasture."

"Oh." That made sense. Logan hadn't said 'you dummy' but he'd seemed to imply it. Or maybe she was being overly sensitive. That was certainly possible.

A few moments later Liam stepped out of one of the stalls. His clothes were a mess, with blood and hay everywhere, but he had the widest grin on his face she'd ever seen.

"Hi, Cici. Sorry I couldn't come get you but Moondance decided to foal. She had a beautiful filly. Would you like to see her?"

"I'd love to."

He led her to a stall at the far end of the barn. "Here comes my mom now." He smiled at her and said, "This isn't how either of us wanted to meet you."

"I think you can be excused. It's not every day your horse goes into labor."

He gestured to the woman walking toward them. "This is my mom. Mom, this is Cici."

"Nice to meet you, Mrs. McFarland."

A petite woman in her fifties with brown hair and a dusting of freckles across the bridge of her nose brushed straw from her clothes. "Please, call me Maureen. It's so nice to meet you, Cici. I'd shake your hand or give you a hug but"—she looked down at her jeans and shirt, which were in the same shape as Liam's—"I can't imagine you'd want to."

Everyone laughed. Liam opened the top part of the stall door so they could see inside. "Meet Moondance and her foal."

"Oh, she's gorgeous!" Moondance was a beautiful buckskin mare. Her cream-colored body and black mane, tail, and stockings were striking. Her foal was a brownish color. She stood on spindly legs by her mama's side.

"Thanks. We think so. We don't know what color her foal will be yet," Liam said. "Foals change color as they grow older. Her sire, Riptide, is a smoky black, so the foal could turn out to be one of several colors."

Logan spoke for the first time since they'd entered the barn. "She's a beauty, Liam."

"She is," he agreed, smiling. "And Moondance is going to be a great mother."

"She already is," Logan said and clapped his brother on his back.

Okay, so Logan wasn't all bad. But he was still annoying.

"Why don't you come up to the house with me and we'll let Liam finish up here and clean up?" Maureen asked Cici.

"Velma made some of her famous sugar cookies and I know she wants you to try them." She paused and added, "You like cookies don't you?"

Cici laughed. "Homemade sugar cookies? Who doesn't like them?"

"Save some for me," Liam said.

"We'll try. Velma always makes a triple batch," Maureen added to Cici.

"Well, you've met Cici now," Liam said to Logan as he made sure the mare had fresh water and hay. The filly looked good and had started nursing. "What do you think?"

"She's pretty." He could say that truthfully, although she was more like gorgeous than simply pretty. Which, of course, made him suspicious. Again. Why the hell couldn't she find a man in Texas?

"That's all you've got? She's pretty?"

"I'm reserving judgment on the rest. She doesn't seem to know much about ranches."

Liam walked over to the big sink and started washing up. "No, she's a city girl."

"Has she told you why she was so anxious to get out of Texas?"

"No. I figure she'll tell me when she's ready."

"I hope she isn't running from a crazy ex. That's all we need is some nut tracking her down."

"Thanks, Logan. You're always so positive."

"Just realistic." He wasn't going to tell Liam, at least not right away, but he intended to find out more about Cici Bradley. And depending on what he found out he'd decide whether to tell Liam or not. He almost certainly would even though his brother was going to be pissed at him. Logan needed to talk to Connor and see what he thought about all this. Assuming Connor knew anything about it. Their brother was a flight paramedic and had been really busy lately.

Liam finished washing up and headed for the house. "Why are you so determined not to like Cici?"

"I'm not. I just think you need to be careful."

"I am."

Doubtful, but Logan changed the subject since it was clear Liam wasn't going to listen to him. "She said she writes thrillers."

"Yeah. So?"

"Have you read any of them?"

"What do you think?"

"I think you haven't read fiction since you left high school."

Liam laughed. "You're right. No, I haven't read her books yet, but I have one of them and I'm going to read it."

"In between your ranch management and horse breeding and all the other crap you read."

Liam stopped walking. "You don't read fiction either. All you read is medical shit."

"I read other things. I read science fiction. And I've read

some thrillers." Not that he could name them since he hadn't actually read a book for pleasure in months. "Does she support herself with the writing?"

"I assume so."

"Damn, Liam, haven't you asked her anything?"

"Ask her yourself if you're so damn nosy," he said, clearly exasperated. "Now I'm going to shower and put on some clothes not covered in blood and hay and then go see Cici."

It seemed to Logan that Liam knew precious little about the woman even though they'd been video-chatting for two months. He hoped his brother didn't regret this.

EARLY THAT EVENING Liam asked Cici, "I know you said it had been a while since you rode a horse, but would you like to take a ride in the morning? I can show you around the ranch a little."

"I haven't ridden since I was a teenager. Do you have a beginner's horse?"

"Of course. Angus is the horse we usually start people out on."

"I don't have any boots. Well, not that I'd ride in. Is that a problem?"

"Do you have tennis shoes? Those will work fine. We can go to town later on this week and get you some cowboy boots if you want."

"That would be fun."

So early the next morning she put on a T-shirt, an older pair of jeans, and her running shoes. She started to leave but remembered Liam's advice to wear sunscreen so she went back for it and a ball cap. She was excited and also a little wary. What if she fell off and made a fool of herself? But Liam knew she was a beginner. He wouldn't expect her to be good. Cici left the house, nearly running into Logan at the kitchen door. "Sorry," she said as he reached out to steady her. "I wasn't looking where I was going." Of course, neither was he. He let her go and they did the sidewalk shuffle, where they dodged the same way several times. Finally she managed to get past him.

"Going riding?" he asked.

"Yes, Liam's going to show me around the ranch."

That was weird. What was that odd little zing I felt when he touched me?

The horse Liam had chosen for her was a big reddish-colored horse. She wasn't up on horse colors so she asked him.

"Sorrel. And Riptide here is a smoky black."

"Oh, right. You said he was the filly's father. He's gorgeous."

"Thanks. Here," he said, handing her a helmet.

"Why do I have to wear a helmet? You're not wearing one."

"It's a rule. Guests have to wear helmets. Especially

guests who haven't ridden in a long time."

She grumbled but she put it on. He was probably right.

He led her out to the round pen first. "This isn't seeing the ranch."

"You haven't been on a horse in years," he reminded her. "This is just until you get used to it again."

It annoyed her, but she couldn't fault him for being careful. After all, she didn't want to fall off and break something either. Before long Liam pronounced her good to go and led her out to a well-worn trail. "This goes past a couple of pastures and then follows the stream before looping back."

They passed the cattle first. "Wow, you have a lot of them."

"Not as many as we used to. I've been concentrating on the horses, but the cattle keep us in business."

"What brand of cattle are they?"

He laughed. "Breed, not brand."

"I knew that." Well, she should have anyway.

"They're Herefords." He went on to talk about the cattle and how he wanted to transition from cattle to purely raising horses, but he knew that was a long way away.

They never went above a walk, which was fine with her. From what little she remembered, trotting was very uncomfortable. Eventually they came to a stream.

They dismounted and ground-tied the horses. Something that, unsurprisingly, she'd never heard of. "So they'll just stay there where their reins were dropped?"

"Yes. Unless there's grass or lots of other horses around. Come on, let's take a walk. We won't be gone too long."

They walked along the stream, chatting about nothing in particular. Then they sat and Liam talked more about his aspirations for his horse-breeding operation. "You really love it, don't you? The ranch, I mean."

He looked at her and smiled. "It's home. When I was younger, before my dad died, I worked in Wyoming for a while. But I missed Marietta. When Dad died my mother needed help, so I came back to help run the ranch."

"When did you lose him?"

"Seven years ago this summer. Farm accident."

"I'm sorry. You must miss him."

"I do. All of us do." He was silent for a moment then said, "My mom is thinking about getting married again."

"Really? How do you feel about that?"

"It's time. Clint is a good guy. He's the rancher who lives next to us," he said with a wave to the north. "They've known each other a long time. Clint's been a widower for several years now."

"So what's the holdup?"

He looked at her as if trying to decide what to tell her. "Apparently, I am."

"I thought you liked him?"

"I do. But my mother won't leave the ranch until I'm settled down. Preferably married."

"Is that why you went to Matchmakers.com?"

"Partly."

Uh-oh. "Um, Liam, I'm not ready to—"

He held up a hand. "I'm not ready either. But I needed to start somewhere. Don't look so worried." He cupped her cheek. "I haven't even kissed you yet." Then he leaned in and kissed her. His kiss was firm, but not pushy. The only things touching were his hand on her face and their lips. His tongue slipped inside her mouth, touched hers and retreated. He drew back and smiled at her.

Oh, damn. The kiss had been nice. Pleasant. Even skillful. But try as she might it didn't spark any fires in her blood. Not that every kiss would, or even should. But still, something was missing. She wondered if he'd felt it too. Maybe once hadn't been enough.

He'd dropped his hand and was simply gazing at her. She had no clue what he was thinking. She put her arms around his neck and kissed him again. Threw more of herself into it this time. He put his arms around her and drew her closer. The kiss deepened. Their tongues tangled. It wasn't bad. In fact, it was nice. Very nice. But it sure as hell wasn't spectacular. They both pulled back and gazed at each other. She still couldn't tell what he was thinking.

Maybe she was expecting too much. And maybe, she thought with a sinking feeling, she was kissing the wrong brother.

Chapter Four

Cici met Connor about ten days after she arrived in Marietta. She'd spent the days before familiarizing herself with the ranch and working on her book. That morning she was in the barn with Liam trying to learn how to groom a horse. She hated to tell him but so far it wasn't her favorite thing to do.

A man came into the barn and yelled, "Liam! Where the hell are you?" She heard him coming closer and apparently stopping when he saw Liam. Cici was on the other side of the horse so she was somewhat hidden.

"Where's the mail-order bride? Is she pretty?"

Liam snorted. "You have no manners. Cici, meet my brother, Connor. Aka the idiot."

She stepped out from behind the horse.

"Oops," Connor said. "Nice to meet you, Cici." His gaze was frankly appreciative. "Just so you know, if you decide you don't want Liam, I'm single." He grinned engagingly. He resembled his brothers except he had blond hair and gorgeous blue eyes. Both Liam and Logan had dark hair. Liam's eyes were hazel, and they seemed to change color with his mood or what he was wearing, and Logan's were a beautiful gray. The three brothers' features were shaped similarly. They were all tall. And hot.

She laughed. "I'm not a mail-order bride."

"That's what Liam told me."

Cici looked at Liam who rolled his eyes. "No, I told you we met through an online dating app."

Matchmakers.com was a dating app but not limited by distance apart. The website boasted of people who'd found someone to marry but after all, that wasn't a requirement. So she didn't say anything.

Connor shrugged. "Tomato, tomahto."

"What do you want?" Liam asked.

"I have next week off."

"I know. You told me you'd help with the horses."

"Yeah, about that. Kayla asked me to go to Las Vegas with her. Just the first part of the week but then I'll be back and can help."

"Who's Kayla?"

"I thought I told you about her. I met her a couple of weeks ago. She's a drug rep. I met her at the hospital."

"Las Vegas, huh? Careful you don't come back married."

Connor laughed. "No danger of that. It's very casual."

Liam turned back to the horse. "Whatever. I'll see you when you get back."

"I'm going to go talk to Mom. I haven't seen her in a while." He paused but Liam didn't say anything. "Nice to meet you, Cici."

"Nice to meet you," she said. As soon as he'd gone she asked, "Are you mad at him? For not staying around to help you?"

"No, that's just Connor. Besides, he'll be here when he gets back from Vegas."

"I know it's none of my business, but have you thought about hiring more help?" As far as she could tell after watching Liam for the last ten days, he had a couple of part-time teenagers who mucked out stalls and things of that sort but if he had full-time help she hadn't seen it. Other than his mother, which made sense as to why she thought he couldn't do without her.

"Yes, I've thought about it. I've had a few who didn't work out. One just recently I had to fire." He grimaced. "It's not that easy to find the right person."

She thought there was a story behind that comment, but she didn't push. If Liam wanted to tell her, he would.

To her surprise he continued. "Before that I had to fire our ranch manager. Found out he was siphoning off money. A little here, a little there. It added up to a decent amount." He paused and added, "At least the hand was just a drunk and not a thief."

"That's terrible. I'm so sorry." No wonder he worked so hard. "Is there anything I can do?"

"Not unless you can magically find an honest, dependable ranch hand and manager." He smiled at her. "But thanks. I appreciate the thought. Enough about my problems. Want to go to dinner tomorrow night?"

"Sure. Where?" It would be nice to go out.

"Do you like Italian food?"

"Who doesn't?"

"I'll see if I can get reservations at Rocco's. Around six thirty okay?"

"Sounds good." She realized she hadn't yet been away from the ranch. This should be fun. Maybe she could get someone to take her to town to shop a little before it. Or maybe she could borrow a car, although from what she'd seen, everyone on the ranch used their vehicles. She needed to get her own transportation, sooner rather than later.

"ARE YOU GOING to the hospital anytime soon?" Liam asked Logan the next morning.

"I'm headed there in about an hour. Why?"

"Would you take Cici when you go? She wants to go shopping and I can't take her. Roland didn't show up this morning and I've got chores to do. That's the problem with hiring teenagers."

Damn, why the hell did Liam ask her here if he wasn't going to take care of her? The more Logan was around the woman the twitchier he got. Which was ridiculous. Sure, she was pretty but besides her being Liam's girlfriend or whatever you wanted to call it, he had nothing in common with her. And what was the deal with Roland? Even Liam's teenage help had been flaky lately.

"I can take her but someone else will have to bring her home."

"I should be able to pick her up. Thanks."

"Think nothing of it," he said sarcastically, which went right over his brother's head.

Half an hour later, Logan called upstairs. "Cici, I'm about to leave." Naturally, she didn't hear him or didn't answer, anyway. So he called again, louder. "Cici, I'm leaving!"

Still no answer. He tromped up the stairs and knocked on her door. She opened it and stared at him inquiringly. "Yes?"

"Liam said you wanted to go into town." She wore cutoffs and a T-shirt, was barefoot, and her hair was in a braid that looked as if she'd slept on it. "You're not ready."

"Oh, crap. I'm sorry! I was writing."

He gazed at her. "And?"

"And I was writing and in the zone, so I didn't realize what time it was. Give me five minutes and I'll be ready to go."

Five minutes? Right. "If you're not downstairs in ten minutes I'm leaving without you."

"Yes, sir," she said, giving him a saucy salute before shutting the door in his face.

To his complete shock, she made it downstairs in five. Clothes changed, hair brushed, and she'd even managed a little makeup. Okay, points for her. "Where do you want to go?"

"Western Wear. Liam said they have boots and clothes."

He grunted in answer.

She was silent until they reached the highway. "Why do you dislike me so much? You don't even know me."

He threw her an annoyed glance. "I don't dislike you." Unfortunately, he was starting to like her too much. He'd tried to avoid her as much as possible, but with both of them living at the ranch he couldn't help but see her often.

"Really? Then why is it whenever we're around each other I feel like I'm having to pull conversation out of you with pliers?"

"I don't like pointless chatter."

"Thanks. I'll try to remember not to chatter pointlessly at you."

"That wasn't what I meant."

"What did you mean?"

"I wasn't trying to insult you."

"Oh, well, that's good to know."

Logan gritted his teeth. "Can we drop the subject?"

"Sure." She looked around for a moment. "What are the mountains called?"

"The ones to the west are the Gallatins. To the east are the Absaroka."

"And your ranch is in Paradise Valley."

"On the edge. We're at the northern end of it."

"I'll be here for a while. Where's a good place to eat lunch? Liam is taking me to Rocco's tonight."

"Grey's Saloon is good. There's also a coffee shop and the Main Street Diner in town."

"I'll try Grey's. Liam mentioned it too."

Logan stopped in front of the Western Wear store. "You'll have to call Liam or Mom to pick you up. I'll be at work."

"I suppose there's no Uber here, huh?"

He laughed. "Nope. No ride share of any kind. We have a taxi service but there's only one car so it takes forever."

"I think I'll need to rent a car. Do you know where I can do that?"

"There's a place just off of Highway 89, right before you get to Livingston. But do you really want to do that?"

"I don't want to drag you and Liam away from work, and your mom needs her car too. So yeah."

He wasn't sure how to ask her if she could afford it without insulting her, so he blew it off, figuring she must not have money problems.

She must have seen his skepticism because she added, "Don't worry. I can afford it."

Cici and Liam seemed to be growing closer by the day. Logan was happy for his brother. He really was. He just wished his feelings for Cici were as brotherly as they should be. But that didn't matter. Cici was Liam's girl, and she was totally off-limits.

Which was probably why he was so intrigued with her. He couldn't have her, so of course he wanted her. The feeling would pass. It had to.

AFTER SHOPPING CICI walked to the library. She'd heard a lot about it. It was in the park, near the courthouse in a gorgeous gray stone historical building built in the 1880s. While she could access most of the research she needed via the internet or online library database, some things required her to go to the library itself. Besides, she was a book geek and loved libraries.

When she walked inside it blew her away. Reading about it simply didn't do it justice. The marble foyer and staircase were complemented by tall windows and high ceilings. The first and second floors were gorgeous hardwood floors that she'd bet were original to the building. Cici, always a lover of libraries, fell madly in love with it immediately. After she'd been there awhile, soaking up the atmosphere, Cici realized one of the librarians was staring at her and finally asked her if something was wrong.

"Oh, no." She flushed. "I'm so sorry. I didn't mean to stare. But…aren't you Cici Bradley?"

"Yes. We haven't met, have we?"

"No. I recognized you from your picture. It's on most of your books."

She'd forgotten about that. Even though she'd published a number of books she was always excited to meet a new reader. "Nice to meet you…"

"Letty. Letty North," she said shaking hands. "And yes, I endure a lot of ribbing since I'm now known as 'Letty the librarian.'"

They both laughed. Cici said, "I promise to never call you that."

"That's okay. I think it's funny too. I read your books and love them. Our library has all of them. Many of them in hardback, paperback, and audio."

"Wow. I'm happy to hear that." It was always gratifying to learn a library carried her books, especially in all formats.

Letty was tiny, with short, dark brown hair styled in a pixie cut, which suited her perfectly. She was also very talkative. Cici really hit it off with her, bonding over a mutual love of books—Cici's and other authors' books. Before she knew it, she'd agreed to give a talk at the library. And she'd made a new friend.

They arranged to meet a few days later at Grey's Saloon one evening for dinner. According to Letty, Grey's was one of Marietta's favorite gathering places. Since she'd be going to Grey's soon she decided to have lunch at the Main Street Diner.

Chapter Five

LATER THAT AFTERNOON, Maureen picked her up and at her request took her to the rental car place. Fortunately, Maureen said she didn't mind staying to show Cici the way to the ranch. She was extremely grateful since there weren't a lot of signs out in the country and although the rental car had GPS, she figured it might be unreliable out here.

Cici had fun trying on her new clothes and deciding what to wear to dinner. Among other things, she'd bought a V-neck cap-sleeve dress that was mostly white with a few red flowers and greenery sprinkled throughout. It hit just above her knees and flared out a little. She'd also bought a pair of beautiful turquoise cowboy boots but she wore them around the house for twenty minutes and decided she'd have blisters for days if she didn't break them in. Besides, they didn't really go with the dress. Instead she wore red, strappy sandals. For a change, she wore makeup and left her long dark hair down. *Liam probably won't recognize me*, she thought with a smile. Most of the time she wore jeans or shorts and a T-shirt, so seeing her in a nice dress would be a change.

"You look great," Liam said when he saw her.

"Thanks, so do you." He wore a pair of gray slacks and a baby-blue shirt that turned his hazel eyes to blue gray. Damn, he was a good-looking man, and a nice one. So why did she keep thinking of a grumpy man who didn't even like her?

Rocco's was a very pretty, romantic restaurant. Dark red leather booths were spaced evenly around the room. Straw-bottomed wine bottles with flickering red candles sat on the tables and the high backs of the booths shut out the other diners and muted much of the ambient noise. There was a beautiful mural of Tuscany painted in pastel golds, greens and blues on the wall beside them. Nearby was a waterfall, the faint sounds of trickling water adding gentle notes to the classical music playing softly in the background.

They talked but it was a little strained at first. Which was odd because they'd never had a problem talking when they video-chatted. Or when she was with him at the ranch, but then, this was a date. Maybe that was it. Then Liam asked her about the book she was working on and the next thing she knew she was telling him about the problem in her plot. After a while she realized his eyes had glazed over and if he was paying attention, she'd eat her brand-new cowboy boots. She shut up and waited to see what he'd do.

"Ah, that sounds interesting," he said after a long pause.

"No it doesn't. You have no idea what I was talking about."

He laughed, not even trying to deny it. "Busted. Sorry, I was thinking about how much it was going to cost to replace the pasture fence."

She laughed too. "I do tend to get caught up when I'm talking books." So she couldn't very well blame him for thinking about something else. "I bet that's pretty expensive."

"It's not cheap but we do most of it ourselves, so the labor costs are minimal, but we're out the cost of the wood."

"You do it by yourself?" Good Lord, that must take forever.

"My brothers help when they can, and I'll hire extra help. But it will have to wait until I sell another horse."

They went back to the ranch right after dinner. Liam asked her if she wanted ice cream, but she turned him down. She knew it was already late for someone who woke up before dawn. At her bedroom door he kissed her. She kissed him back. And damn it, it happened again. Nothing. No zing, no zip, nada. Just…pleasant.

"See you tomorrow," he said, and left her.

Well, he certainly wasn't pushy. She wondered if he was taking it slow or if he simply wasn't all that attracted to her. It should hurt her feelings, but it didn't. Probably because she felt the same way.

"You're up late," Logan said to Cici when he walked into the living room a few evenings later. He hadn't expected anyone to be up since he knew Liam turned in early, but he hadn't known Cici stayed up late. She looked up from her computer, her gaze unfocused. She sat in the recliner with the footrest out and her computer on her lap, looking like a child in the huge chair. On second thought, not a child, but she sure was tiny.

"I thought you were working."

"I was. I came home after my surgery."

"Liam said you stay at the hospital usually when you're on call."

"Depends." Tonight he hadn't because he wanted his own bed and he wanted to not think about his last surgery, which was hard to do if he stayed at the hospital. Who was he kidding? He knew damn well he would think about the surgery, and if there'd been anything he could have done differently. No matter where he was. The only thing that could take his mind off his worries was sex, and that obviously wasn't happening tonight. In fact, he hadn't been with a woman in far too long. For some reason he'd lacked the interest and energy it would take to date someone new. He shook off that thought.

Deciding that talking to Cici—or anyone, really—was preferable to being alone, he sat on the couch.

"What are you doing?" he asked, although it was obvious. She wore knit pajama pants and a T-shirt that had seen better days with a faded logo that read: *Watch it or I'll put you in my novel.*

"Writing. Liam went to bed and I'm a night owl so I figured I'd try to get some writing done. I came down here for a change of scene." She studied him for a moment. "Is something wrong?"

"Why do you ask?"

"For one thing, you're talking to me. For another you seem different. Sad or something."

How had she recognized his mood? Most people couldn't read him when he was upset, even his family. "I've talked to you before."

"Not much, and then only when necessary."

He shrugged and didn't reply. She was probably right.

"Do you want to talk about it?" she continued.

"Talk about what?" The woman was entirely too observant.

"Whatever's bothering you."

He didn't want to talk about it. What was the point? But she'd caught him in a weak moment. A moment when he wondered if talking about it might help him. Most of the time he kept things to himself. Surgeons couldn't show weakness and that's what he figured his inability to accept that he couldn't save everyone was. A weakness. What the hell. Maybe he should try it. "I lost a patient tonight."

"I'm sorry. That must be hard. Was it expected?"

Logan shook his head. "He was thirty-eight, with a wife

and a two-year-old. It was a freak accident. His tractor overturned and crushed him."

"Oh, my God. How awful."

"I had to call in another surgeon. Samantha Gallagher and I—she's one of the trauma surgeons—operated for hours. I thought he was going to make it. But he didn't. He'd lost too much blood and had too many injuries." And he'd had to tell the family. One of the worst parts of his job. He'd lost patients before. It was unavoidable. But something like this, when the man had been so young and had so much to live for…it got to him. "My dad—" He cleared his throat and started again. "That's how my father died. An accident with his tractor."

Cici set aside her computer, got up and came over to the couch. She sat beside him. Put a hand on his shoulder and patted him. "I'm sure that made it doubly hard."

It had. He'd known it even though he hadn't acknowledged it until now. Farm accidents were common, but not many of them involved a tractor overturning, just as it had happened with his father.

"I'm so sorry. I wish I could do something to help."

He turned his head and looked at her. She was so close, her expression so sympathetic, her gaze meeting his and holding. Her eyes were brown. Not ordinary brown but a deep, rich chocolate, shot through with gold highlights. He'd never seen anything like her eyes. She was close, close enough to kiss. He wanted to kiss her. Who was he kidding? He wanted more than that.

Holy shit, what am I doing? She's Liam's girl.

Hastily, he scrambled up. "I—uh, I have to go. Thanks for listening." And he got the hell out before he did something unforgivable. Like kissing his brother's girl.

CICI WATCHED LOGAN leave, wondering what had just happened. That had been weird. And close. For heaven's sake, she'd almost kissed Logan. Or he'd almost kissed her. She'd seen the desire in his eyes. Worse, she'd felt the urge too. What would it be like to kiss that hard mouth, to feel it soften, to have his tongue dip inside and—

Shit, I'm so not doing this.

She'd kissed Liam, but only a couple of times. The most recent just two days ago after dinner. It had gone no further and to be honest, kissing Liam hadn't been all that exciting. They'd been nice kisses but there had been no spark. For her, anyway, and she didn't think Liam had felt much either. He sure hadn't acted as if he did.

Why? She liked him. He was a good guy. Lord knows he was hot. So why did she feel nothing more than a mild interest in Liam? Whereas with Logan… Whenever their gazes met she felt the pull, the desire to explore more. Sometimes she didn't even have to look at him to feel the attraction. And she absolutely could not act on it.

Besides, Logan was just having a bad night. She'd probably misinterpreted what had happened. Logan didn't even like her.

She'd never really thought about what it must feel like to a doctor when he or she lost a patient. After all, she wasn't in the medical field, and she hadn't ever lost anyone close to her. She'd gotten the impression that Logan kept a firm grip on his emotions, and rarely spoke as he had tonight. It made sense. No one wanted a surgeon who wasn't in control. She'd wanted to console him. To make him feel better, but she hadn't known how.

He'd left. Practically ran out of there as if he was fleeing a fire. Which, if she was honest, was undoubtedly a good thing. She and Liam weren't together, but they were supposed to be giving it a shot. He'd paid her way out here and was putting her up and feeding her. Meanwhile she was lusting over his damn brother.

Not cool. Not a person she wanted to be. She needed to talk to Liam before anything happened between her and Logan. Not that it would because neither she nor Logan would let it. She was probably overreacting but still, she owed it to Liam to be honest. Oh, not about Logan, but that she felt no more than friendship for him. But she needed to be sure before she told Liam there was no hope for them to be anything more than friends. And she wasn't sure.

She trudged upstairs, got in bed, and turned out the light. She lay there, tossing and turning and trying to get

Logan McFarland out of her mind. She wasn't very successful.

When she finally fell asleep she dreamed about him.

WHEN SHE WALKED into Grey's to meet Letty for dinner, she saw a long bar along one wall with people sitting on barstools or standing in front of it. The decor was rustic, with dark wood and brick, and it suited the place perfectly. There were pool tables and darts, and a tiny dance floor where a solitary couple were slow dancing to a fast song.

She looked around and saw Letty waving at her from a booth. A pretty redhead sat across from her. Letty got up and hugged her before introducing the woman with her. "Cici, this is Mia Gallagher. Mia, this is Cici Bradley, the writer I was telling you about."

"Nice to meet you," Cici said, shaking hands.

"Nice to meet you, too."

"I thought you might like to meet some more people since you're new to town," Letty said. "Mia is married to Wyatt Gallagher, who is an orthopedist at the hospital. She's an artist. You can see some of her paintings in the local businesses."

"Did you paint that beautiful landscape at the western wear store?"

Mia looked pleased. "I did. I'm glad you liked it."

"I love it. I'd love to see more of your work."

"Anytime. I have a small gallery on the edge of town. Drop in whenever you like."

They chatted more and Mia said, "Letty's been raving about your books. I haven't read any yet but I'd like to. I haven't had much time for reading recently. But I'm hoping I'll have some soon. What would be a good book to start with?"

Cici and Letty spoke at the same time, naming the first book in her latest series. "It's great," Letty said. "But don't read it late at night when you're alone. I had to go get a bat for protection and turn on every light in the apartment for the next two nights. I still couldn't sleep well."

Cici laughed. "Not sure that's a great endorsement, Letty."

"Thrillers are supposed to be thrilling. And scary and suspenseful. Yours are all three."

"Thanks, Letty," she said, touched.

"Why thrillers?" Mia asked her. "I mean, why do you write thrillers rather than another genre? And did you always want to be a writer?"

Cici laughed. "No, I had no idea what I wanted to do but I did like writing. It wasn't until I worked in a law office as a receptionist that the writing bug bit me. The cases I read about sparked my interest and I started reading a lot of true crime books, thrillers, and mysteries. Then I read a newspaper article that gave me the idea that turned out to be my first book. It was pretty awful and I submitted it everywhere. Which, naturally, horrifies me now. But I kept writing new ones and eventually I sold one."

"I can't imagine writing a book," Mia said.

"I can't imagine being able to paint," Cici told her. They both laughed.

"Each to her own," Mia said. "Speaking of that, I can't help being curious about why you decided to go the online dating route." She looked her over and added, "I mean, it's not as if you're ugly or anything."

Cici laughed. "Thanks, I think. You know how hard it is to meet people when you're our age. People you'd like to date anyway."

"True. But why go so far away?"

"At first I didn't intend to. But the app I used specialized in finding people who don't live in the same area. And I'd had some bad experiences in Fort Worth so I was ready to leave. For a while, anyway. And then I met Liam." She paused and added, "You've *seen* Liam, right?"

Mia and Letty both laughed. "Good point," Letty said.

"He's definitely hot," Mia agreed. "But then, there are a lot of hot guys in Marietta. Including my husband, naturally."

They laughed and Letty said, "She's not kidding. You'll see when you meet him."

"Are you from Marietta?" Cici asked Mia.

"No, I moved from Denver. Wyatt and I knew each other there and after he'd been here a while, he asked me to visit. We've been married four years now and we have a three-year-old son. He's starting preschool soon and I can't wait."

"Is he a handful?"

Mia grinned. "Yes, he takes after his father. Who happens to be taking care of him tonight."

Cici learned about the rest of the Gallaghers, a large clan who all happened to live in Marietta. While Letty joined in the conversation Cici noticed she didn't mention her own family.

"Does your family live in Marietta, Letty?"

"My parents passed away my senior year of high school and I'm an only child. I grew up here and other than going to college in Wyoming, have lived here all my life. I lived with the Fletchers my senior year until I turned eighteen."

"I'm sorry for your loss," Cici said.

"Thanks. It's been a long time."

"The Fletchers meaning Liam's best friend Riley and his family? The ones who live on the neighboring ranch to the McFarlands'?"

"Yes. Val Fletcher is one of my best friends. I'll introduce you sometime."

By the end of the evening Cici had gotten to know Letty better and made another friend in Mia. She was beginning to feel right at home.

Before she first started corresponding with Liam she'd

thought about moving but she hadn't decided where. The dating app had been more of a whim than anything else but the more she talked to Liam the more Marietta interested her. He sent her pictures of the town and told her stories about it. And he sent pictures of the ranch and his obvious love, his horses. It sounded so appealing. As did the idea of getting out of Texas, even if only for a short time.

But the longer she stayed in Marietta the more she realized she could be happy here. As for her past, she knew she'd have to come clean about it at some point but she couldn't do it yet. Not when it could ruin what she was beginning to have in Marietta. A home. Happiness. Friends.

And love?

Chapter Six

LOGAN WOKE SEVERAL days after his midnight talk with Cici knowing he had to do something. He'd dreamed about the damn woman. Every night. Woken up hard for her. Cici. Liam's girl. God, he was such a dick.

Logan met Connor at Grey's Saloon after work. Connor was late—no surprise there. But Logan went ahead and ordered him a beer and took it to one of the booths. He didn't want to move. Not really. But staying in the same house as Cici was becoming impossible. Once he got away from seeing her constantly this fascination with her would end. Wouldn't it? Damn it, it had to.

Connor slid into the booth across from him. "Thanks," he said, picking up his beer and taking a healthy swig. "I can only stay for one beer. I have a date later."

Unlike Liam and Logan, who both had dark hair, Connor was a bit of a throwback. He took after their maternal grandmother who'd been blond with blue eyes and if rumors were true she'd been a real firecracker. Connor was the eternal bachelor and totally satisfied with that existence. Well, Logan had been too, he just didn't have the rep that

Connor did.

"Who is it this time? It's not Karen is it?"

"Karen?" he said as if he'd never heard of her. "Oh, Karen. Nah. She kicked me to the curb last week. It's Marcie, one of the radiology techs." He drank more beer.

"Marcia."

He shrugged. "Yeah, her."

Logan shook his head. Connor liked women. All women. Luckily for him, women liked him right back. Logan was pretty sure he'd never settle down. Not that Logan blamed him. It wasn't until lately that Logan had considered settling down. He just hadn't found a woman he could imagine trusting that much. Especially not given his previous experience with serious or, at the least, exclusive relationships. Until…until he'd met his brother's girl, damn it.

"Liam couldn't come?"

"I didn't ask him."

"Okay." He rubbed his nose. "Why not?"

He didn't answer that directly. "I'm thinking about moving into town."

"You mean leave the ranch? Why?"

He trotted out the standard "So I can be closer to the hospital."

"So after three or four years you've suddenly decided you don't like the drive? Sorry, bro, that won't fly. What's really going on?"

Connor had a big mouth but he wouldn't talk about

something like this, something that would hurt Liam. Nevertheless, he warned him. "This is just between you and me."

"Okay. Now you've really got me curious. What's up?"

"I can't be at the house all the time with Cici there."

Connor rolled his eyes. "I know you don't like her but—"

Logan snorted. "If only. The problem is, I like her too much."

Connor's eyebrows rose. "Damn, Logan, that's not good."

"Tell me about it."

"You haven't done anything, have you?"

He glared at his brother. "Hell, no. I wouldn't do that to Liam. He thinks he's gonna marry the woman."

"I didn't know they were that serious. Has she been flirting with you? Because if she has—"

"No, nothing like that. She and Liam—hell, I can't tell what exactly is going on. Obviously they like each other but I'm not sure they're even sleeping together."

Connor looked confounded. "That's the first thing I'd have done."

"I'm aware," he said dryly. "But Liam isn't like that. Or maybe it's her. Maybe she wants more time to get to know him."

"Let me get this straight. You want to move because you have the hots for your brother's girl."

He started to protest but then he shrugged. "Pretty

much."

"Oh, man. What are you going to do if they decide to get married?"

"I'm sure this is a temporary thing. If I don't have to see her all the time it will just die a natural death." He hoped. Or he'd remain obsessed but at least he wouldn't be living with them, seeing the two of them together daily.

"Are there any apartments for rent at your complex?" Connor lived at the Absaroka apartments, across from the elementary and middle schools. They were nothing special, but they were decent and near the hospital.

"I haven't paid any attention, but probably."

"I'd planned on buying a house in town, but I just haven't gotten around to it. Liam needs to get some full-time help. You and I aren't able to help out as much as he needs. Maybe if I move, he'll realize he has to find someone."

"I know, but he's gun-shy since the last two he hired were shitty." Connor paused and drummed his fingers on the table. "This puts more work on Mom too."

"If he manages to get Mom to marry Clint and move out, he'll have to find someone. He should have done it long ago and maybe then he wouldn't have had to resort to a matchmaking service."

"So you still think this is all because of Mom? Because he wants her to marry Clint?"

"So he says."

"I think there's more to it. I think he's lonely."

"Maybe," Logan said. "But he's convinced that there aren't any women around here who don't know about Caroline. Which is why he's hooked up with Cici."

"I thought you said they haven't hooked up yet?"

"I didn't mean it literally." Although they could be lovers and he just didn't know it. Quickly, he shook off that thought. He was doing everything he could to avoid thinking about that.

"Good luck telling the family. Neither of them is gonna like this idea."

"I know. But they'll just have to deal with it." Because he was going to go absolutely fucking nuts if he didn't get away from there soon.

CICI WATCHED LIAM for a bit as he groomed Riptide. The horse was beautiful, and master and horse clearly loved each other. She'd thought the first time she'd watched Liam ride his horse that the two of them moved as one. They made a picture, all right. Hot man, beautiful stallion, beneath a gorgeous blue Montana summer sky. By rights she should have been completely taken with him.

But…she wasn't. Liam was one of the nicest men she'd ever known. But try as she might, and she had tried, she felt nothing for him beyond friendship. Honestly, she wasn't sure how he felt about her. She suspected he felt no more for her than she did for him. He certainly didn't act as if he was falling for her. He hadn't made another move since kissing her, most recently on the Fourth of July. Of course, she'd told him early on that she wanted to take the physical part slow, so maybe he was just heeding her wishes. But really, there was slow and then there was glacial. And she and Liam were definitely the latter.

"Hey," she said, walking forward.

Liam looked up from Riptide and smiled at her. "Hey. Taking a break?"

She'd told him she planned on writing today. Which she had until she got too distracted by her own thoughts, and those thoughts were not about the book, either.

She nodded. "Can we talk?"

"Uh-oh. That sounds serious. Let me finish up and we can take a walk."

"Okay. I'll wait outside."

A short while later Liam left the barn and found her on the path to the closest pasture. "So," he said as they began walking, "what's up?"

She wasn't sure what to say. Or how to start anyway. "I've been here a while now."

"Nearly five weeks, give or take a few days."

"I think it's time for me to move out."

He looked surprised. "You want to go home?"

"No, I was thinking of staying in Marietta."

"And you don't want to stay here. Why?"

She hesitated. "I like you, Liam."

"I like you too."

"But I don't think you and I are ever going to be more than friends. One of the reasons I came here was to see what we thought after getting to know each other and maybe settling down. And I just don't see that happening."

He didn't seem upset. In fact, he wore that expression she'd seen on occasion when he didn't want people to know what he was thinking. The 'aw-shucks-ma'am-I'm-just-a-simple-cowboy' look that she knew for a fact hid a sharp mind. She'd figured that out early on from their online conversations before she ever met him in person.

"You don't have to leave."

"I can't stay here. It wouldn't be right."

"Why?"

"You know why," she said, exasperated. "I'd be staying under false pretenses. We said if it didn't work out, I'd leave."

"You don't have a place to stay and your car is a rental, which is costing you a fortune," Liam pointed out.

She put her hands on her hips. "Obviously, I'll have to find a place to live and buy a car." And sublet her apartment or get out of the lease altogether.

"Or you could go back to Fort Worth."

Not a chance in hell. She loved being somewhere that no one knew the sordid story of her parents and their scheme. "I like Marietta. Will it be a problem for you if I stay?"

"You mean because of my broken heart?"

She sent him a dirty look. "If you've got a broken heart this is the first I've heard of it."

He laughed, swung an arm around her shoulders and hugged her. "My heart's not broken but if we'd kept going it might have been."

"I don't think so. I'm not your type."

"What is my type?"

"Someone who loves and understands ranches and horses for one thing."

He was quiet for a long time. Finally she asked, "Liam, are you okay?"

"Yeah, I'm just thinking. Would you mind not telling anyone what we decided? At least for a while?"

"Why?"

"I told you about Mom and Clint. And that she won't marry him until she believes I'm settled. That I have someone to help me with the ranch and preferably someone I'm in love with."

"If I move it puts the kibosh on that idea, doesn't it?"

"Yeah. Unless I can figure something out. I could hire a manager and that might be enough. Of course, it's not that easy to find the right person for the job. It's not like I haven't been looking. So far the two I hired were awful. One was a crook and the other didn't know his head from his ass. And finding a full-time hand isn't easy either."

"Even if you found a manager it doesn't do you much

good finding a woman, though."

He shrugged. "It might be enough to convince her to go ahead and marry the guy. And we wouldn't have to pretend forever. Just for a little while."

"I don't know, Liam. Maybe you should just tell her the truth."

"That hasn't worked so far."

"I'm not the only woman in the world, you know. Isn't there someone around here you could be interested in?"

"No. Which is why I did that stupid Matchmakers.com thing. Someone who wasn't from around here seemed like a great option. I should have known it wouldn't work."

She didn't know why he was so adamant about not finding a woman around the area. But then she hadn't told him her reasons for leaving Texas either. "You could try again."

"Why bother? I have the perfect woman right here and it's not gonna work out."

She laughed. "The perfect woman? You've got to be kidding."

"Well, I'm not. You're smart, you're beautiful, you're a nice person—"

"You're sweet, but you're not in love with me. And even though you're smart, kind, and damn good-looking, I'm not in love with you."

"Maybe we haven't given it enough of a chance."

"I don't think that's it, and if you're honest, neither do you."

He shrugged, not denying it. "So will you stay?"

"I don't know, Liam. Let me think about it. Are you going to talk to anyone? Tell them what's going on?"

"No. Why would I?"

"I thought you might want to talk to your brothers."

"Are you kidding? Connor has a big mouth so he's out. And I don't want to hear I told you so from Logan. He thought this idea was crazy from the first."

"Is that why he doesn't like me?"

"Logan doesn't dislike you."

"Could have fooled me. But never mind that. Give me some time to think about this. But I'll tell you one thing, I need to buy a car regardless of what happens. I'm thinking of volunteering in town somewhere part-time. It might make me more productive with my writing."

"Time away will make you more productive? That doesn't make sense."

"Maybe not but it usually works." And in the meantime, she needed to decide whether to go along with Liam's plan or not. There were pros and cons, of course. But the main reason she figured she'd do it was that Liam was a nice guy and she didn't want to leave him in the lurch. Which is exactly what would happen if she moved out.

Chapter Seven

LOGAN SHOULD HAVE known it wouldn't be easy to move out without having to explain and argue about his decision to everyone and his dog. First, he told his mother, who was baking cookies in the kitchen. Sugar cookies, from what he could tell. Unsurprisingly, Maureen was not happy with him.

"What about Liam?" she asked. "You know he depends on you to help when you can."

"Hell, Mom, I'm not moving out of the state. I'm only going to town. I'll still help Liam. He needs to hire more help anyway."

"Well, of course he does. But I still don't understand why you want to leave. Why now?" The oven timer dinged, and she grabbed a hot pad to take the cookies out of the oven.

"Mom, I'm thirty-four years old. It's time I had a place of my own. Besides, if Liam and Cici get serious they won't need me hanging around."

As she took the cookies off the pan and slid them onto wire racks she said, "I'll still be here."

"We all know Clint wants you to marry him." He started to grab a cookie but Maureen slapped his hand.

"They're still too hot."

"I like them warm."

She rolled her eyes but let him grab one. "I'm not so sure it's going to work out between Liam and Cici."

"Why?"

"Just a feeling I have."

Maureen's 'feelings' were famous for being right more often than not. "I thought you liked her."

"I like her very much. That doesn't mean they're right for each other."

"Have you told Liam that?"

"Of course not. He's a grown man. He'll have to decide for himself whether they suit or not."

Yeah, he wasn't going to hold his breath on that one.

After he left his mother he tracked down Liam. His brother was out in the round pen with one of his new mares. She was a beautiful bay he planned to breed soon. "She's looking good, Liam." He climbed the fence and sat on the top rail.

"Yeah. She's a sweetheart too."

"I need to talk to you."

Liam glanced at him. "About what?"

He saw no reason to beat around the bush. "I'm moving into town."

Liam didn't speak for a long moment, letting the mare

circle the pen. "Why?"

"I want to be closer to work."

"Is that the only reason?"

"What other reason would I have?"

Liam shrugged.

"I'll still be around to help when I'm off." He didn't want Liam to think he was deserting him.

"Don't worry about it. I'll manage. I need to hire more help anyway."

True, but he hadn't managed it so far. Maybe this would force him to try again. Surely everyone he hired couldn't be as bad as the last two. "You're pissed."

"No. I figured you'd move at some point. I'm kind of surprised it took you this long."

"I'm going to get an apartment while I look for a house."

"What will you do with Rambler while you live in an apartment?"

Shit. He hadn't thought that through. Rambler was Logan's dog, unlike the other seven who more or less belonged to everyone on the ranch. Not long after Logan returned to practice in Marietta he'd found the German shepherd mix as a puppy someone had abandoned in the hospital parking lot. Rambler wouldn't be happy in an apartment. He needed a place to run. In fact, Logan wasn't sure how much he'd like a yard rather than the ranch.

But Rambler was also devoted to Logan and wouldn't be happy without him. Damn. "He'll have to stay here until I get a house with a yard. If that's okay with you." Maybe the dog would be okay as long as Logan visited him regularly.

"Of course. He's lived here most of his life. But you'll have to come see him as often as you can. And take him home with you occasionally. You know how he frets when he doesn't see you for days at a time."

"Don't worry. I'll take care of him." He loved the dog. He was so accustomed to him being around he hadn't thought about the logistics of living in an apartment with an eighty-five-pound dog who was used to living on a ranch.

"I think Cici is more of a dog person than a horse person," Liam said.

"She doesn't like horses?" That wasn't good. Liam and his horses were inseparable.

"No, she likes them. But she seems more drawn to the dogs. Rambler, especially, is crazy about her."

Logan hadn't noticed. But then, he'd spent a lot of time avoiding Cici.

"Are we done?"

"Yeah. I meant what I said about helping you when you need it."

"I know you did. Don't worry, I'll call you. And by the way, I have an interview with a ranch manager tomorrow. The day after that a new hand is starting."

"Really? Why didn't you tell me that first thing? What made you do it now?"

"I needed to and I'm getting ready for Mom to leave.

Although I'm not sure she's going to do it anyway."

Yeah, neither was he. "Do you think the new people will work out?"

"Who knows? I think the hand will. He's worked on ranches before and is new to the area. As for the manager, who knows? I'm going to keep a close eye on him."

"Hope they both work out."

HEARING THAT LOGAN was moving out had really rocked Cici. According to Liam, he wanted to be closer to the hospital. Which was reasonable except...why now? She'd agreed to stay at the ranch and continue to let everyone think she and Liam were still together. She wasn't sure how long that would last. She knew Liam wanted it to last as long as it took him to convince his mother to marry Clint and move to his ranch. Liam had also told her he'd hired new help and was hoping they worked out.

What if Logan was moving because of her? Or rather, because of her and Liam. Because he thought she and Liam were getting serious so he needed to get a place of his own. And of course she couldn't ask him because to do that would break Liam's confidence.

Cici managed to keep her mouth shut until the day Logan moved. He was at the bottom of the stairs with a large box, heading toward his SUV. "So I guess you found an apartment," she said brilliantly.

"Yeah. At the Absaroka, where Connor lives." He set down the box and swiped his arm across his forehead. Moving was sweaty business.

"What are you doing with Rambler? Is he going with you?"

Logan frowned. "I'll bring him to visit but he wouldn't be happy living there without a yard. I'm hoping I can buy a house soon."

"He'll miss you. So will Liam." *So will I.*

He gave her an enigmatic look. "They'll survive." He hesitated then said, "Could you do me a favor?"

"What?"

"Give Rambler some extra attention. He likes you and—" He shrugged.

"Of course. I like him too." *And unfortunately I like you way too much.* "Liam doesn't want you to move."

"He hasn't said anything."

"Does he really need to?"

Logan shrugged again. "It's for the best. Besides, I'm only moving into town. It's not like I won't ever be here at the ranch. I'll still be here to help Liam."

Sure he would, but if he was anything like he'd been lately he'd be avoiding her like the plague. "I might see you at the hospital."

He looked startled. "Why? Are you sick?"

"No, I'm starting as a volunteer next week."

"At the hospital? What about your writing?"

"It's for research on a book. At least partly. I've volunteered at a number of places for research, but I haven't been at a hospital yet. Besides, it's just a few hours a week. I'll still have plenty of time to write."

"I thought you wrote every day?"

"Most days. But I keep weird hours. Which you know since you found me downstairs at one a.m. the other night." When he simply stared at her she added, "You know, the night you came home after your patient died."

"I remember," he said.

So did she.

"I never thanked you for that."

"I didn't do anything."

"Yes, you did. I needed someone to talk to and you were there." He picked up his box. "I'd better get moving."

"Good luck."

"Thanks."

And with that he walked out the door. He was only moving into town. Why did she feel like he was moving out of her life?

Because he was. He felt something for her. She was almost sure of it. But since she was Liam's girl, or he thought she was, he wouldn't do anything about it. And neither could she as long as she was supposed to be with Liam.

Damn it.

Chapter Eight

LOGAN WAS BEAT. He'd operated most of the day and while that wasn't unusual, for some reason today he was extra tired. Thankful his shift was over, he got on the hospital elevator. He heard a "Hold it!" and stuck an arm in the door to keep it open.

Cici got in and said a breathless thanks. Logan knew she'd been volunteering at the hospital, but this was the first time he'd run into her there.

"Hi, Logan."

"Hi." Damn it, why couldn't he get over his stupid obsession with her? He hadn't yet, anyway. It didn't matter how many times he reminded himself she was Liam's, he still wanted her. And there wasn't a damn thing he could do about it. If Cici had been the type to cheat on his brother he wouldn't want her. But she wasn't. Besides, there was no way in hell he could make a move on his brother's girl. But he wanted to. Damn, he wanted to.

"Are you off work?"

He nodded. "Heading home."

"I'm heading out too. Are you liking your new apartment?"

He shrugged. "It's okay. I'm planning on buying a house so I hope I won't be there long."

"Do you miss the ranch?"

He missed seeing her, but he couldn't say that. "Sure, sometimes. My room was a lot more comfortable. And I wish I could have Rambler with me. I hadn't realized how much he was with me until I moved."

"What about Liam and your mom?"

"What about them?" Where was she going with this?

"I just wondered if you were sorry you moved."

Was he? He didn't miss the drive in the middle of the night, but since he often stayed at the hospital when he was on call, he hadn't done that terribly often. It was undoubtedly better that he didn't see Cici all the time but…he missed her. Which was stupid.

The elevator stopped with a lurch. The lights went out and after a minute or two the emergency lights came on. "Shit," Logan said.

"What happened?"

"We're stuck in between floors."

"Stuck? Won't the power come back before long?"

"Maybe. If we're lucky. Last week someone was stuck between floors for hours. The elevator was supposedly fixed after that, but obviously it wasn't."

Cici punched the buttons but nothing happened. She pulled out her cell phone. "No bars."

Logan walked to her side, picked up the elevator phone, and held it to his ear. "Great. It's out too."

"Wonderful. Do you suppose all the elevators are stuck?"

"No way to know."

"What do we do?"

"Wait."

"What about your pager? Can you contact someone with it?"

"No. I only receive messages. I can't send them."

She made a frustrated sound. "Why doesn't the elevator phone work? I'd think they'd have to keep it working."

"They try. This elevator is squirrelly. Always has been." He sat on the floor, propping his back against the wall. "You might as well sit. It might be quick, but it could also take hours to restore the service."

"Hours? Great." She was dressed casually in jeans and a sweater with a T-shirt beneath it. Her hair was pulled back in a ponytail and it didn't look like she had much, if any, makeup on. And he thought she looked great.

"Why are you frowning at me?"

"I'm not. I'm frowning at the situation."

She seemed to make a decision. She sat beside him and said, "This has gone on long enough."

"What are you talking about?"

"For the life of me I can't figure out what I've done to make you dislike me."

Not this again. "I don't dislike you," he said sharply.

"I've told you that several times."

"I know. But I don't believe you." He didn't speak and she continued. "If you're not avoiding me, which you do whenever possible, you're frowning at me like I've done something horrible."

Annoyed, he glanced at her. "You're being paranoid."

She raised an eyebrow. "It's not paranoia if they really are out to get you."

Frustrated beyond belief he said, "Damn, Cici. Give it a rest. I don't dislike you. If anything it's the opposite."

She sucked in a breath and stared at him.

Well, fuck. Now he'd done it.

CICI STARED AT Logan. Surely he hadn't meant… "The—the opposite?"

"Forget it. I didn't—just forget I said anything."

"I can't. Did you mean it? You don't hate me. You said 'if anything it's the opposite.' Which means… You like me? Or…you have feelings for me?"

"You're committed to my brother. What I feel doesn't matter."

"What if Liam and I weren't committed to each other? It's not like we've made an announcement or anything."

"You're living at the ranch. At Liam's invitation. In my book that means you're involved with each other. Do you really think I'd hit on my brother's girlfriend?"

"No." Of course he wouldn't. And she couldn't contradict him without betraying Liam's confidence.

He glared at her. "I didn't take you as the cheating type."

"I'm not," she said. It wouldn't be cheating but Logan didn't know that. "There's nothing official between Liam and me. We're still getting to know each other."

"Semantics. You're involved with my brother. Period. End of discussion."

The elevator jerked and she fell against him. His arms encircled her, hesitant at first, as though he was simply propping her up. But then his hold tightened, becoming firm. Their gazes met. His gaze fell to her mouth, then back up to her eyes. *Oh, my God. I must be dreaming. Logan looks like he wants to kiss me.*

No. She had to be wrong. He couldn't. More importantly, he wouldn't. Not when he thought he'd be betraying his brother. But then his head dropped until his mouth was inches from hers. Her heart pounded; her pulse raced.

The elevator jerked again, then halted. Muttering an oath, Logan released her and she scrambled to her feet. She'd thought she was the only one who felt something. But unless she was very much mistaken, Logan felt something too. For her.

She'd told Liam they could pretend to be involved until his mom got married or, at least, agreed to get married. And he didn't want to tell either of his brothers that they weren't truly involved. But instead of going away, her feelings for Logan had only intensified once she and Liam had agreed they wouldn't suit.

She'd fallen for the wrong brother. She'd realized it almost from the first. Liam deserved a woman who loved him wholeheartedly. A woman who understood him in a way she couldn't. She liked the ranch. She liked horses. But they weren't her life, like they were Liam's. She wasn't destined to be a rancher's wife.

As soon as she got back to the ranch she was going to talk to Liam and tell him they needed to let Logan know the truth. But what if it caused a rift between the brothers? Just because Liam didn't want her didn't mean he'd be okay with her turning around and falling for his brother.

The McFarland brothers were close. Did she want to be the reason they lost that closeness?

THE DAMN ELEVATOR was still stuck. With his luck they'd be trapped for hours. Not that Logan wouldn't have liked the time alone with Cici in another situation. Like one when she wasn't involved with his brother.

"It's hot," Cici said, sitting down again.

"That's what happens when the air conditioner goes out."

"It's just weird. The hospital is always so cold I have to

go around dressed for winter whatever the weather."

"It might help if you took off your sweater."

She did so and he wished she hadn't. Beneath the bulky sweater she wore a short-sleeved fitted T-shirt. It probably wasn't meant to be sexy but it was. It showcased her breasts and her trim stomach, and tucked into jeans that were worn, old, and tight. Or at least, they looked old with their ripped knees. He wasn't up on women's fashion but he realized he'd seen a lot of women and girls wearing jeans with rips and holes in them. Weird.

He needed to get out of the damned elevator. He'd almost kissed her. Again. What was wrong with him? He didn't do shit like this. He'd been burned before when his high school girlfriend cheated on him with one of his former friends. Of course she'd lied about it until she was caught, literally, with her pants down. They'd both lied to him, and he'd believed them, until he'd had no choice but to see the truth. God, he hadn't thought about Janelle in forever. He'd just as soon never think about her again. They hadn't been serious, but they'd been exclusive. Or so he'd thought.

And then there'd been Beth during his surgical residency. They'd been serious. And that had blown up in his face. She hadn't cheated on him but she'd sure as hell lied. He'd thought she was smart. She was. He'd thought she was honest. She wasn't.

He closed his eyes and leaned back against the elevator wall. He tried to think of anything but his exes but unfortunately, all he could think about instead was Cici.

"What are you doing?" Cici asked.

"What does it look like? I'm trying to sleep."

"Sorry. I forgot you don't like pointless chatter."

He cracked open an eye. "Don't take it personally."

"Kinda hard not to."

He knew he was being an ass. It wasn't Cici's fault they were stuck, or that he couldn't stop thinking about her. He quit pretending to sleep. "Why did you leave Texas?"

"I thought you didn't want to chatter."

"Deflecting much?"

She didn't speak for a long moment. "Something bad happened and I wanted a fresh start somewhere else."

That made sense, but damn, it was a long way to go. "So bad you had to move completely out of the state?"

"Yes. And that's all you need to know."

No, it really wasn't. But he also knew she wasn't going to tell him any more.

She pulled a small notebook and a pen from her purse and started scribbling.

"What are you doing?"

She ignored him at first and he didn't think she was going to answer at all. Closing the notebook, she said, "I had something occur to me about my book and if I don't write it down I'll forget it. I've tried putting it in my phone before and that doesn't work as well for me."

Half an hour later they finally started moving again. He

wasn't sure who was more thankful to get out of that elevator. "I'm going to head back to the ranch," Cici said.

"Okay, I'll walk out with you." They walked out the doors and he started to follow her to the lot. It was in the opposite direction from where the doctors parked.

"You don't need to walk me to my car."

He ignored her. "It's late. It's no big deal." There wasn't much crime in Marietta but that didn't mean it was nonexistent.

When they reached her car, she unlocked her door and turned around. "Thanks. I'll see you around."

He nodded. "Yeah." He started to walk away but he heard the car make the rumbling sound that meant the battery wasn't cranking enough to turn over. He stopped and waited to see if it would catch. It didn't. In fact it quit rumbling and started clicking. He walked back and tapped on her window. She opened the door.

"Need a jump?"

"Apparently. It's been hinky lately. I should have gotten it checked out."

"I'll go get my truck. Do you have jumper cables?"

She looked guilty. "Um, no. It isn't brand new but it's not old and I just bought it. How was I to know they sold me a car with a bad battery?"

"Not a problem. I've got them. But you really should carry some with you," he couldn't resist adding.

"Ya think?"

He laughed and left her. When he returned and they tried to jump her battery it became obvious that it was dead. Not ailing but totally dead. "You're not going anywhere in that car tonight. You'll have to get a new battery in the morning. Come on, I'll take you home."

"I can ask Liam to come get me."

"Why, when I can take you now?"

"I don't want you to have to go to the trouble. I'll just call Liam."

"You realize he's probably asleep or nearly so."

She frowned. "Sometimes you're very annoying."

"I get that a lot. Get in the truck, Cici."

"Fine. But I should still let Liam know. I told him I'd be back hours ago."

Logan's phone rang. He saw it was Liam and answered. "Hey, we were just about to call you."

"We?"

"Me and Cici. The elevator got stuck between floors and once it finally got going Cici's battery died. I'm bringing her home."

"Good. I was getting a little worried, but I figured maybe she was with friends and forgot to tell me. I appreciate you helping her out and bringing her home."

"No problem." He wouldn't appreciate it if he knew how close Logan had come to kissing her. Of course, she might have simply punched him, which would have served him right. "By the way, have you had the road fixed yet?" The dirt road to the house was in bad shape and getting worse. Every time he drove it he thought of that but tonight it seemed even worse. One good rain and it would be impassible.

"Not yet. I had to bring the barn's sprinkler system up to code first. And the road's going to cost more than I'd planned on, so I haven't done it yet."

"Connor and I can pitch in."

"No."

That was it. Just 'no.' Damn his brother's pride. "Don't be stubborn. At least let me pitch in. I lived there until a few weeks ago. It's my responsibility too."

"We'll talk about it later. I'll see you when you bring Cici to the ranch. And thanks for offering."

He knew he was in for a fight with Liam about the road. Once Liam made up his mind, it was damn near impossible to change it.

Chapter Nine

A SHORT TIME later, Cici was seated in Logan's big gray pickup. She'd argued with him, but he wasn't budging. He was driving her to the ranch, period, end of discussion. She'd had to practically vault to get in since the pickup had no running board and was high off the ground. He'd offered to help her but had backed off when she glared at him.

"I'm sorry you have to drive me out to the ranch but I'm guessing there's nowhere open to get a new battery tonight."

"If there is I don't know of it."

"Still, I should have asked Liam. He's obviously awake."

He turned his head to stare at her. "What's going on? Do you not want to be alone with me that badly?"

"Don't be ridiculous," she said, though it was the truth. "I hate to make you drive all the way out to the ranch and then have to come back."

"I did it for years."

"For work."

"I have this feeling there's more to it than you not wanting to put me out."

That was the truth. Being alone with Logan for all that

time had tried her last nerve. There was no future for her with Logan. Even if he was interested in her he wouldn't act on it. He *might* if he knew she and Liam were no longer together, and they were only pretending for Maureen's sake. Not that she and Liam ever had been really together. But as it stood now she needed to forget about Logan. If only she could.

"What was that about the road?"

"You've probably noticed it's in bad shape."

"Hard not to."

"It's expensive and a pain to fix. Filling the potholes only works for so long."

"What happens in the winter? When there's tons of snow on that road?"

"Liam keeps it plowed. He's got a blade for his truck."

"So he has to plow the road too, besides all the other stuff he does? He needs more help."

"Tell me about it," Logan muttered. "When I was around I did it sometimes."

"Yes, but you're gone now. What's he going to do this winter?"

"He's working on getting help. Told me he had interviews with a ranch manager and a new hand, but I haven't heard how it went."

"Do you ever get snowed in?"

"Occasionally. But if we are, then so is everyone else."

"I don't think I'd like that."

"Nobody *likes* it. You just have to cope with it. It's not that big a deal." He turned to look at her. "You don't know much about Montana, do you?"

"Just what I read after Liam invited me here. I'm not used to snow. We don't have a lot where I lived in Texas. We had Snowmageddon one year and it shut down half the state. Everything was frozen, power was out, and it lasted for days."

"It never snowed much when I lived in Dallas."

"Where did you go after medical school?"

"I stayed in Dallas for my surgical residency too."

She was suddenly glad he didn't know her real last name. Had he been around when the shit hit the fan with her parents and their scheme? He could have heard about it. Damn, she didn't want to have to go through all that again. The notoriety she'd lived through had nearly broken her. And she sure as hell didn't want Logan, or Liam, or anyone else to think she was a crook like her parents. Which was why she should probably have told Liam. But Liam was so easygoing he'd never asked much about her past so she hadn't volunteered it.

"Did you get over to Fort Worth any?"

"A few times. Mostly I worked. And if I wasn't working I was sleeping."

"That sounds…brutal."

He shrugged. "It was, sometimes. That's just the way a surgical residency is."

"Why did you move back to Marietta? Was that always your plan?"

"No. I thought I'd go somewhere else but the hospital here grew enough to need more doctors. And Mom and Liam needed help with the ranch. So I came back."

They turned onto the road to the ranch. At the gate Logan asked her, "Will you drive the truck through while I get the gate?"

"Sure."

He got out of the truck. Cici climbed over the console to sit in the driver's seat. He opened the gate and she drove through, put it in park and climbed back over.

A short while later they pulled up to the garage. Liam had told her it was a fairly recent addition. Originally the house hadn't had one, but his parents had added one shortly before his father had died.

Logan punched a button on the truck and the garage door rose. "Take care."

"Aren't you coming in?"

"No, I need to get back."

"Oh, well, thanks. I appreciate you going to all this trouble."

"Not a big deal."

She watched him go until he was out of sight. She had to talk to Liam. She couldn't keep this secret any longer. Not from Liam. She wanted to get to know Logan. Wanted the freedom to be with him—assuming that's what he wanted.

Their talk in the elevator had gone a long way to convincing her that Logan was interested in her. But he was too dang honorable to go after his brother's girlfriend. Which was a good thing. Right?

A FEW DAYS after the 'elevator incident' as Cici thought of it, she still hadn't told Liam about her feelings for his brother. They weren't going away. In fact, they'd only grown stronger. She owed it to Liam to tell him how she felt. Particularly if she wanted anything to ever happen with Logan. Deciding she'd procrastinated long enough, she found Liam down by the nearest pasture. At the moment Moondance and her foal were the only ones in it. He was leaning on the fence watching them.

"That's a pretty picture," she said as she walked up. The hot guy wasn't so bad either. Why she couldn't have fallen for him was a mystery to her.

He turned and smiled at her. "Yes it is. What are you up to?"

"I thought we could maybe take a ride and talk."

He cocked his head. "Talk. About anything special?"

"I'll tell you on the ride."

A short while later they were cantering down a lane that led to the creek. It was Cici's favorite ride. She had to admit she enjoyed riding again and had actually gotten decent at it, but it also was something she could live without. Not so with Liam. From what she'd seen Liam would go crazy without access to his horses. She knew he did a lot of other things to maintain the ranch, such as oversee the farming and cattle operations along with his mother, but the horses were his true love.

Damn it, life would be so much easier if she'd just fallen for Liam. But then, he hadn't fallen for her either so that would have sucked too.

After reaching the creek they both dismounted and walked along the water, leading the horses. "So, what's this about, Cici?"

She sucked in a breath and began. "It's about our situation. Pretending we're falling for each other. I know we agreed we'd keep up the pretense until your mom agreed to marry Clint and move, but…" Great. What was she going to say now? She should have thought this through better but really, how do you tell the man you're currently pretending to be in love with that you're terribly afraid you've fallen for his brother?

"You want to call it off?"

"Not exactly. I know you're depending on me." And honestly, she felt as if she owed it to him. Not that he'd done anything to make her feel that way, but she knew he'd been out a tidy sum flying her in and putting her up. And he'd already refused to let her pay him back. "I wondered if we could tell someone else. That it's not for real, you know?"

He stopped walking and gazed at her for a little while. She couldn't tell what he was thinking, but he didn't look angry. "Have you fallen for someone, Cici? Is that what this is about?"

"Not exactly. But I've been thinking about…someone else. Of course, I haven't done anything or said anything since I'm supposed to be with you."

He rubbed the side of his nose. "Does he have feelings for you?"

"I don't know. But I do know he won't do anything if he thinks we're together."

"That's a good sign, at least. Can he be trusted to keep his mouth shut until we decide to break up or do we just need to call it quits now?"

"I think he'd go along with it if we told him we aren't a couple and why we're pretending. Except, I don't even know if he's interested in me that way."

"Do I know him?"

"Yes. Very well, actually." Liam just looked at her and waited. "It's um, it's Logan."

Eyes widening, Liam stared at her. "Logan? Logan, my *brother Logan* has been hitting on you? Are you shitting me?"

"No! Of course he hasn't. He wouldn't do anything to hurt you. But I have feelings for him and unless he knows there's nothing going on between you and me I'll never know what his feelings are."

Liam said nothing.

"At first I thought he didn't like me but he got over that. We've talked some and well, I think he could be interested. Or maybe I'm wrong, but I'd like to find out."

"Damn, Cici, I don't know what to say."

"Don't be mad at Logan. He has no idea about any of this."

Liam shook his head. "I need some time to think about this. Do you have to know right away?"

"No. And if you think we should keep him in the dark then I'll respect your wishes."

They rode back after that, neither of them talking. She couldn't tell what Liam was thinking. She hoped she hadn't hurt him, but she suspected she had. Even if he wasn't in love with her it was bound to be unsettling, at the least, to have his pretend girlfriend tell him she'd fallen for his brother.

After taking care of the horses, Liam stopped her with a hand on her arm. "Hold on a minute."

He pulled her close and laid a kiss on her that was definitely not just a friendly kiss. Damn, the man knew how to kiss. He lifted his head and smiled at her. "Nope."

"Nope?"

"Just checking."

"Checking?"

"Checking if we were wrong. But it's still not there, is it?"

No, damn it, it wasn't. "It would make life easier if we

had fallen for each other."

He released her and began walking away. "It would."

"Liam?" He turned and looked at her. "You're a really good kisser."

He laughed and walked off.

Chapter Ten

After stripping off his gloves and gown following his last operation, Logan found a message from Liam on his phone.

LIAM: *I NEED TO SEE YOU ASAP*
LOGAN: *WHAT'S UP?*
LIAM: *JUST GET OVER HERE*
LOGAN: *WORKING. CAN'T COME UNTIL TOMORROW MORNING.*
LIAM: *FINE*

That was definitely odd. Liam didn't like texting but he did it occasionally. Logan couldn't say why because after all, it was texting, but he thought Liam seemed pissed. Oh well. He'd find out in the morning.

The next day Logan found his brother in the barn, of course. Putting fresh wood shavings in the stalls after mucking them out, which was supposed to be their part-time helper's job. "Where's Kirk?" He was the new teenager Liam had hired.

Liam leaned on the shovel he'd been using to spread the

shavings and wiped his arm across his forehead. "Went out of town with his parents."

That was the problem with teenagers. They had their own lives. "Are you about finished?"

Liam walked out of the stall and put up his shovel. "Yeah." He went to the sink and washed and dried his hands, then turned around, crossed his arms over his chest, leaned back against the sink, and pinned him with a decidedly unfriendly look.

"What's this about and why are you looking at me like you want to skewer me?"

"I'm trying to decide whether I need to beat the shit out of you or not."

"You and who else?" Logan answered automatically. They were very evenly matched; at least, they had been the last time they went at it. But that was years ago now and Liam lived an extremely active life, involving a lot of heavy-duty physical work. Whereas while Logan worked out and helped at the ranch some, it didn't compare to what his brother did daily.

"Just me." He eyed Logan suspiciously. "I hear you've been hitting on my girl."

"What? Where the hell did you hear that?"

"From Cici."

"What the hell? Why would she say that? I've never touched the woman." But he'd thought about it. A lot. "Jesus, Liam, you should know I wouldn't do that to you."

Liam nodded. "That's what Cici said."

"What? That I hit on her or that I wouldn't?"

"That you wouldn't."

"Then why the hell did you accuse me of hitting on her?"

He shrugged. "I wanted to see how you'd react."

"Why? What's the point of that?"

"Cici wants me to tell you that she and I are faking it. We're pretending to be together so that Mom will marry Clint. Except it's not working. So far, anyway. Mom hasn't mentioned a thing about it."

"Wait. You—you're not in love with Cici?" Holy shit, he never expected this.

"Luckily, no. I'm not."

"Luckily? I don't get it. Why not? She's smart, she's beautiful and—What the hell are you grinning about?"

"Don't you wonder why Cici wants you to know the truth about us?"

"None of this makes sense to me."

"Cici told me she had 'feelings' for you," Liam said, making air quotes. "And the more I think about it, the more I think you have 'feelings' for her too."

"Why would you think that?" He'd thought he'd kept his 'feelings' for Cici to himself.

"I've seen the way you look at her when you think no one sees you. Kinda like you're a man dying of thirst but the only water around isn't for you."

Logan opened his mouth but nothing came out. He

cleared his throat. "That's ridiculous. I don't." Damn, that was probably an apt description.

Liam raised an eyebrow. "Keep telling yourself that. At any rate, Cici agreed to keep up the pretense for a while longer. Hoping we can convince Mom to move out."

"Does Connor know?"

"Are you kidding? No, he doesn't know."

"Did you sleep with her?"

Liam smiled. "I don't kiss and tell. Ask her if you want to know. Not that it's any of your business." He left the barn, leaving Logan standing there feeling like a fool.

Shit. He knew he had no right to question Liam, much less be upset if they had slept together. Liam had been thinking about marrying her if they were compatible. And what better way to figure that out than to sleep together?

It shouldn't bother him. After all, she was in her late twenties. It was extremely unlikely that she was a virgin. He wasn't. Why should she be? No, it wasn't the fact that she'd slept with somebody before him that mattered. It was the 'who' that bothered him. His brother.

AFTER LIAM LEFT Logan stayed in the barn to think things over. He didn't know what to do. Cici wasn't involved with Liam. His brother swore he wasn't in love with her. She'd told Liam she had feelings for Logan. He had to admit Liam and Cici had certainly never been ones for PDA. But that didn't mean there wasn't something between them.

Before Liam's confession that they were faking it, he'd tried to convince himself he wanted Cici simply because he couldn't have her. That hadn't worked. Then he'd tried to convince himself he simply needed to get laid. He'd had several opportunities, but he hadn't taken one. He didn't want another woman. He wanted Cici. And now Liam had basically told him to go for it. But how? He couldn't date her since she and Liam were ostensibly together and his mother knew lots of people in Marietta. If someone saw them together she'd be sure to find out. She'd tear Logan a new one if she thought he was cheating with his brother's girl. And she'd almost certainly let Cici have a piece of her mind as well. Logan winced thinking of that.

"Logan? Liam said you wanted to see me." Cici stood in the barn doorway, looking a little uncertain. She wore tight jeans that hugged her curves and a short-sleeved T-shirt with a picture of two little girls on it. One whispered to the other, *She's a writer.* The other one whispered, *Oh, I thought she was just weird.*

He couldn't help smiling. Then he grabbed her hand and pulled her with him into the tack room, shutting the door behind them. "Logan?" She tried to drop his hand but he kept hold of hers.

He didn't know how to approach this other than coming right out and saying it. "Liam said you and he aren't together. You're just faking it to get Mom to marry Clint."

"Yes. I um, asked him to tell you."

"Why?"

"Don't you know?"

"Liam said you had feelings for me. He thinks I have feelings for you."

"Is he right?"

He cupped her cheeks and kissed her. He meant it to be sweet and easy, but she opened her mouth and her tongue stroked his and fire exploded between them. She put her arms around his neck and wrapped herself around him. His hands fell to her waist and pulled her closer. She made a needy sound that almost made him lose control. Damn, you'd think he was a kid who went from simmer to a rolling boil in an instant. Before he could completely devour her he made himself pull back. But he didn't let go. They stared at each other and then they both smiled.

"I guess that's a yes." She'd left her hair down. It looked soft and silky and he wanted to bury his hands in it while he kissed her.

"I thought you didn't like me. But ever since you said 'if anything, it's the opposite' all I've been able to do is think about you."

"I can't stop thinking about you either. I had to remind myself you were Liam's girl every single day. It's been driving me crazy."

"Is that why you were always so crabby to me?"

"It was that or kiss you, and there was no way I'd do that to my brother."

"I know. I wanted to tell you, but I'd promised Liam we'd wait to tell anyone we decided we weren't going to work out. He still thinks he can get your mom to marry Clint before we have to come clean."

"I think he's dreaming." He let go and sat in the chair, then pulled her over to sit in his lap. "She's not going to do that until she's sure Liam doesn't need her anymore. Personally, I think he just needs to hire more help, which he says he's doing, but Mom is convinced he needs a wife."

"Your mom is amazing. I can't imagine having a mother who'd put her own happiness aside for her grown son."

"She's a great mom. Always has been."

"You're lucky."

"I take it that's not your parents."

She laughed without humor. "Hardly. They were totally self-centered from the time I was a teenager. Maybe younger."

He rubbed her back. "That's hard. Do you still see them?"

A closed look crossed her face. "No. They're not in my life anymore."

"That bothers you, doesn't it? Do you wish they were?"

"I wish they were different people. But they aren't so I have to deal with reality."

"Sounds like there's a story there."

"Not one I like to talk about."

"Then don't. It's not my business."

"It's an ugly story."

"Is it why you left Texas?"

"Partly. Let's not talk about it now."

"Okay. What did you want to talk about?"

She wrapped her arms around his neck. "Talking wasn't what I had in mind," she said, and kissed him.

"Is it weird that I feel guilty?" Cici asked Logan some time later.

"If it is I'm weird too."

"Really?"

"Yeah. I have a hard time believing Liam hasn't fallen for you. Especially because I did about five minutes after we met."

"You did not. You didn't like me at all."

"I was completely gobsmacked. And I couldn't show it. I shouldn't have even been thinking it."

What else could she do but kiss him again? She threaded her fingers through his hair. It was dark brown, closer to black really. Short, but thick and silky. She wondered if he knew he had amazing hair. She leaned forward and kissed him, tentative at first but then he took it deeper. His tongue delved in her mouth, and she met it with hers. It was even better than the first time. Or the second. A kiss shouldn't affect her so much. But kissing Logan was like no other kiss she'd ever had. The taste, the heat, the pure passion. She'd never felt anything like it, even with Randall, her boyfriend who'd broken up with her when the shit hit the fan. She'd thought she might love him but his kisses had never made her dizzy with wanting him. And when he'd dumped her at the first opportunity she hadn't missed him. Not one bit. Angry, yes. Missing him, no.

Still dazed, she said, "We should probably go. We don't need your mom walking in on us."

"I locked the door."

"What did you plan to do if someone came and beat on the door?"

"Tell them to go away."

Cici laughed. "Not sure that would work. I don't know how we're going to see each other until Liam and I officially break up."

"We'll have to figure out a way. God knows how long Mom will take to agree to marry Clint. Poor guy has been sweet on her for years."

"Hasn't he gotten tired of waiting?"

"I'm sure he has. But the alternative is losing her, and he obviously doesn't want to do that."

"Are you sure they both want to get married?"

"I think so. We've all asked her about her feelings for Clint at one time or another. She admits she cares about him but she says she isn't ready. Sometimes I wonder if there's a reason she's delaying—other than Liam—but if so she won't talk about it. They've been friends a long time. He lost his wife about a year before we lost Dad. I guess it was natural they turned to each other. And Clint's a great guy."

Cici wondered what it would be like to have both a mother and a father you could love and admire. As much as she hated what they'd done she still loved her parents. But she'd realized even before she'd blown the whistle on them that they hadn't ever loved her. No, that was wrong. She believed her father loved her. As for her mother, Cici wasn't sure she was capable of truly loving someone besides herself. To be fair, she hadn't been a terrible mother. But for as long as Cici could remember she was never the daughter her mother wanted.

"I wish I could take you out. Have a nice, romantic dinner somewhere, even just take a walk together."

"But we can't."

"No, but you could come to my apartment. I could pick up takeout."

"How? I can't park my car there. Someone would see. I've already discovered that you can't hide much in Marietta."

"Park at the hospital. I'll pick you up there."

"What if someone sees us there?"

"I took you home when your battery died. You weren't worried then."

"That's different. We weren't—we hadn't—Oh, never mind."

"We'll have to be careful."

She hadn't considered any of the difficulties when she'd convinced Liam to tell Logan their secret. She'd only known that she couldn't keep her real feelings secret from Liam any longer. It wouldn't have been fair to him. Liam wasn't in love with her any more than she was with him, but he still deserved the respect of her telling him how she felt about his brother.

Logan and she couldn't have an open relationship. Not at this point. Sneaking around didn't suit either of them but if they wanted to see each other they had no choice. And it wouldn't be forever. She knew Liam was working as hard as he could to get his mom to marry Clint. "All right. When?"

"This afternoon. I'm off until tomorrow morning."

"I can't stay with you overnight."

"Why not?"

"You know why not."

"Yeah, I guess you're right."

But someday she could.

Chapter Eleven

CICI FOLLOWED LOGAN up the exterior stairs to his apartment. The Absaroka apartments were an older complex that was close to the hospital. He opened the door and said, "I haven't done anything to make this place look better since I'm planning to move as soon as I find a house. That's also why I don't have much furniture."

Much was an exaggeration. The apartment was very sparsely decorated. There was a couch that had seen better days, a coffee table, and a very large flat-screen TV that dominated the room. It made her laugh. It was such a guy thing to have.

Cici realized she was nervous. She and Logan didn't know each other well. They hadn't talked nearly as much as she had with Liam. But when they had talked she'd felt a connection to him. And every time she looked at him she wanted him.

"If you keep looking at me like that we're not going to make it to the bedroom."

His words sent a thrill through her, but she still felt compelled to ask, "Are you sure about this? About you and me?"

He slipped his arms around her waist and kissed her lightly. Even that brief kiss had a kick to it. "I'm sure. Are you?"

"Yes." She hesitated. Logan had to wonder, even though he hadn't asked her and she didn't think he would. "There's something I want to tell you." He looked at her and waited. "Liam and I... We never slept together."

"It's none of my business but I'm glad to know that." He pulled her close and kissed her. Leaning his forehead against hers, he said, "I really want to make love to you, Cici. But if we're moving too fast just tell me."

"I feel like I've been waiting forever. Which is silly, I know. We haven't even known each other that long."

He gave her a slow smile, swept her up, and carried her into his bedroom. "Long enough to know what we want." He set her down beside the bed. "I've wanted you since the first time I saw you at the airport."

"No, you didn't. You didn't even like me," she said, repeating what she'd told him earlier.

"I liked you too much. And you were Liam's girl so I knew I was screwed from the get-go."

"I tried not to like you. Not to want you. And there was Liam who was everything I should have wanted. But I didn't. I wanted you."

He kissed her slowly. Their tongues touching, sliding against each other. Tangling. Almost immediately the kiss turned hot and fast. Her breasts tingled; she throbbed between her legs. He helped her pull her top over her head. Put his hand on her lace-covered breast. "Pretty." He reached behind her and undid her bra. It fell down her arms, her breasts spilling out. Her nipples were already hard points. Logan sucked in a breath. "Gorgeous." He bent his head and sucked a nipple into his mouth. She groaned and arched into him.

"Take off your shirt," she demanded.

He yanked it off over his head. Cici ran her hands over his bare chest. Muscles. Sleek, not bulky. She knew he worked with Liam and suspected those muscles came as much from ranch work as a gym.

He unbuttoned and unzipped her jeans, pushing them down over her hips. She kicked off her shoes, pushed her jeans all the way down and stepped out of them, one leg at a time. Wearing only her panties, she sat on the bed and watched him as he quickly stripped off the rest of his clothes, taking jeans and underwear off at the same time.

He sat beside her, took her in his arms and kissed her again. He played with her breasts, cupping them, running his fingers over her nipples, then plucking them. Then he pushed her back on the bed and took a nipple in his mouth, sucking on it until it hardened, then moved to the other one. Wanting more, she arched up, pressing her breast to his mouth.

She put her hand on his cock and stroked it. Logan

groaned. "Better not unless you want me to go off right now."

She smiled and stroked more. "Really?"

"Really. And I have things I want to do first." He grabbed the hand in question and placed it above her head. His other hand dipped beneath her panties and he slid one finger inside her.

"Oh." She moaned and he kissed her, swallowing the sound.

He continued to stroke her, his finger going in and out, his thumb rubbing her clit. She bucked beneath his hand, then raised her hips to urge him on.

"You're wet," he said, his voice gravelly.

"Yes."

"For me."

"Yes," she said again. "I want you, Logan."

He didn't reply with words. He continued to stroke and caress her. First kissing her lips, then moving down to torment her breasts with his mouth, and his hand that wasn't driving her to oblivion elsewhere.

She gasped his name, so close to the edge she knew she'd come any second.

He grabbed a condom and fit it over himself. Cici held out her arms, welcoming him as he covered her. She kept her eyes on his as he entered her slowly, stretching her to the limit. "Okay?" he asked.

"Better than okay," she gasped as he pulled out and

drove inside her. He did it again. She wrapped her arms and legs around him and held him tightly. She was close, so close to her climax but she couldn't quite reach it. Until he reached between them and rubbed her clit and she exploded with a cry. He pumped inside her again and again. She felt him stiffen and he poured himself inside her with a harsh groan as his orgasm overtook him.

He rolled off her and held her for a long moment before getting out of bed and going to the bathroom. He came back shortly after and took her in his arms, cuddling her against his chest.

For the first time in a long time, Cici felt content.

AFTER WEEKS OF telling himself he couldn't have Cici, he finally had, and it had been even better than he'd imagined. Logan knew it was way too soon, but he could imagine a future with her. A thought that should have scared the shit out of him but didn't.

He wasn't sure how long he and Cici could keep their relationship secret but they only had to do it until his mother relented enough to marry Clint. Or Liam gave up that line of attack. Liam seemed to think he could convince her to do it soon, but Logan wasn't so sure.

Someone knocked on his door. He debated not answering it. The only person he was interested in seeing was already here with him.

"Logan, open up. I saw your truck. I know you're home."

Damn, why did Connor have to pick tonight to come over? Connor was the odd son out in the looks department. He took after their maternal grandmother with his blond hair and blue eyes. Both Liam and Logan looked like their mother, at least to the extent that they both had dark hair. "Go away, Connor. I'm busy," he said through the door.

"Open up. I won't take long."

Logan knew Connor wouldn't give up until he at least opened the door. Cici was back in his bedroom but she could come out at any moment. He cracked open the door. "What do you want?"

"Hello to you too. I need to talk to you."

"Ever heard of a telephone?"

"You weren't answering." He took in the fact that Logan was wearing jeans and no shirt. "You've got a woman here. No wonder you wanted me to go away."

He didn't deny it. What was the point? "So talk," he said, still blocking the doorway.

"Logan, do you want me to call in a pizza?"

Oh, shit. He turned his head and saw Cici in his living room, wearing one of his button-down shirts and most likely nothing else. She looked gorgeous, sexy, and very much like she just got out of bed. With him.

Connor's expression clouded. "That sounds like—" He

shoved open the door and stepped inside. "Cici."

Shit. Damn. Hell.

Connor looked at him incredulously. "What in the everlasting hell are you doing? Cici and you?" He turned to Cici. "I thought you were decent. I thought you were good for Liam. Obviously I was wrong. I had no idea you were a two-timing s—"

"That's enough!" Logan cut him off. "It's not what it looks like."

"Right. You're not screwing your brother's girl. Damn, Logan, it was bad enough when Caroline left him at the altar for another man. But for you—his own brother—to screw him over—literally. Damn you." Connor's right hook came out of nowhere.

"Shit." Logan wiggled his jaw. He thought about punching back but given what Connor believed, with complete justification, he couldn't blame him. "It's not like that," he repeated. "Sit down and I'll explain."

"I'll stand," Connor said, crossing his arms over his chest and glaring at both Cici and Logan.

"I'll be back," Cici said, and left the room. Hopefully to put some clothes on. Not that he minded seeing her in nothing but his shirt, but he didn't want his brother ogling her.

"Give me a reason why I shouldn't tell Liam that you're a complete piece of shit."

"He already knows. About me and Cici I mean."

"Oh, right. Liam doesn't care that you're screwing his girl."

"Stop saying that, damn it. She's not his girl and I'm not—"

"What? If you're not screwing her then what's she doing wearing your shirt and looking like she just rolled out of bed?"

"Liam and I aren't together," Cici said, entering the room wearing her jeans and T-shirt. "And he knows that Logan and I are, and he's okay with it. But your mother doesn't know and you can't tell her."

Connor scowled and looked at Logan. "What does this have to do with our mother?"

"Everything," Logan said.

Connor stared first at one then the other. Rubbing a hand over his face, he sat on the couch and said, "Somebody tell me what the hell is going on."

They told him the whole story, sometimes Logan and sometimes Cici speaking. Logan admitted it sounded somewhat crazy, but he couldn't help that.

When they finished Connor shook his head. "This is too convoluted not to be true. I know Liam wants Mom to marry Clint, but does he really think he can convince her to do that by pretending to be ready to marry Cici?

"Yes."

"Do you believe that?"

Logan shrugged. "Not really but it's worth a try. Besides,

it's Liam's and Cici's decision and that's what they've decided to do."

"I'm not going to let Liam down," Cici said. "I'll do whatever he asks of me. I feel like it's the least I can do."

"You're sure Liam is okay with you dumping him for Logan?"

"I didn't dump him for Logan. We made a mutual decision that we weren't going to work out. We had decided that long before Logan and I got together."

Connor looked skeptical. "What do you two plan to do if Mom figures out you're together? You think *I* was mad, she'll rip your face off, Logan." He looked at Cici. "God knows what she'll do to you."

"She won't find out," Logan said. "We're being careful."

"Famous last words."

"As long as you don't blow it, we'll be fine."

"I can keep my mouth shut."

"Since when?"

"Ha ha. Don't worry about me. Worry about yourselves."

He would, Logan knew. But the only way to avoid worrying completely would be to avoid Cici and that was something he really didn't want to do.

Chapter Twelve

"Logan, I'm so sorry," Cici said after Connor left. "I didn't realize someone was at the door. I should have been more careful."

"You wouldn't have heard him knocking. There's no way you could have known. Don't worry about it. Connor won't say anything."

"You said he had a big mouth. So did Liam. That was one reason he didn't want to tell Connor the truth."

"Connor won't say anything that would hurt Liam."

"I hope he won't." She paced the room. It was so small she couldn't pace but a few steps before having to turn around. "This is a bad idea."

"What's a bad idea?"

"You and me." She gestured between them. "Sneaking around like this. We should wait until we can be together without hiding."

"Is that what you want?"

"No, but it's what we should do. It would only be temporary."

"If we have to wait for Mom to decide to marry Clint we

could be waiting forever."

"We have to at least give Liam a chance for his plan to work."

"What happens if it doesn't?"

"I don't know. We'll figure that out if we need to." She'd only just found him. She didn't want to stop seeing him. But they'd been naive to think they could carry on an affair without anyone knowing. Thank goodness it had been Connor who discovered them together and not someone else.

"I want to be with you. I don't want to stop."

"Oh, Logan, neither do I. But we owe it to Liam. And your mother."

Logan pulled her close and kissed her. A kiss that soon had her wanting more. She moaned. With his lips still locked on hers, he boosted her up. She wrapped her legs around his hips. He started walking to the bedroom.

She pulled her mouth away. "Logan, we can't—"

"Yes we can. If this is the last time I get to be with you for God knows how long, then I'm going to make love to you again. Once wasn't nearly enough."

She stripped off her shirt as he carried her. "I'm not going to argue with you." She dropped her shirt; her bra followed. He groaned when she pressed her bare breasts to his naked chest.

"I dreamed about you. I felt guilty every time I did but I couldn't help it. No matter how many times I told myself you weren't for me, my mind and body disagreed."

"I dreamed about you too," Cici said. "But the reality is—" She kissed him and then continued. "So much better."

They fell on the bed together. Cici unzipped her jeans and pushed them and her panties down her legs, kicking them off. Logan had stripped off his jeans while she took care of hers. She thought it would be fast and wild, but Logan had other ideas.

He grabbed her hands, holding them with one of his and stretching them above her head. "Slow down. I'm going to explore every bit of you." His lips traveled down her neck, across her chest to her nipples. He took one in his mouth and licked it, smiling as it peaked. He suckled it leisurely, drawing it deep into his mouth until she squirmed, then moving to her other breast to do the same thing.

His hand slid over her stomach and kept going until he sank a finger inside her. How could she still want him as much—more—than the first time? He added a finger and she gasped. "Logan."

He rose above her, pushed her legs apart, then put her legs over his shoulders. Her eyes widened, the position making her vulnerable, open. She watched as he rolled the condom over his shaft. His gaze held hers as he entered her with a single thrust. Deep, so deep, she could hardly tell where she ended and he began. He pushed inside even deeper, pulled out and drove inside her again. And again. And again, until she felt nothing but delirious sensation rocketing through her.

She came, crying out his name, heard him rumble her name and felt him pulsing inside her as his orgasm overtook him.

A FEW DAYS later Logan met Connor at Grey's Saloon for a beer. Luckily he'd been working since he last saw Cici. Thank God for work where he had to concentrate on his patient and the operation and couldn't afford to let anything else intrude. Downtime was limited too. But he was off for the next two days and wasn't sure how long he could resist seeing her. Both of them had agreed it was best not to see each other while Cici was supposed to be with Liam. Too much risk.

They'd talked on the phone and video-chatted and, while it was nice getting to know her better, it was torture not being able to hold her, touch her, make love to her.

They'd had sex twice. It wasn't enough. He was hooked on her. At first he'd wondered if the fact that she was Liam's, and therefore unattainable, had been why he was so stuck on her. But actually being with her had blown that idea clean out of the water. His feelings for Cici had nothing to do with his brother.

"Damn, Logan. I've been talking to you for five minutes and you still haven't heard me. You've got it bad," Connor said, taking the seat across from him and grabbing his beer.

Connor was right. Logan hadn't even heard him. "Do you think Liam's right? That if he can convince Mom he's serious about a woman she'll marry Clint?"

Connor thought about that for a moment. "No. I'm not sure she wants to marry Clint."

"Really? They've been together for a long time now. I know he wants to marry her. And she seems crazy about him." Logan thought about the times he'd seen Clint and his mom together. They laughed and joked and even finished each other's sentences at times. He knew his mother cared about Clint, but did she really love him?

"Something's holding her back. And I don't know that Liam is all of it. Or even most of it. I think he might be a convenient excuse."

"You might be right," Logan said. "I hadn't really analyzed it. But Liam does need help. You and I can't do enough. Why the hell can't he hire someone?"

"He has. But not a ranch manager. He's gun-shy since the last two people he hired were so bad." Connor picked up his beer and drank.

"Can't really blame him for that. But he needs several hands too, and hiring the two he did isn't enough. Stubborn bastard thinks he can do it all himself and he can't. Not if he wants to grow his horse business or even keep it running. I don't think you and I realize how much Mom does to help. But she must realize it."

"Maybe it's money," Connor said. "Does he talk to you about business? He doesn't to me."

"Not really. Every time I offer to chip in on something, like fixing the damn road, he turns me down."

"Me too. But back to Mom, seems to me she could have married Clint long ago if she'd really wanted to."

"Maybe she doesn't really want to marry Clint but she doesn't want to lose him totally. If that's true then Liam's idea that if he's just settled down Mom will marry Clint sure as hell won't work. I'm not sure how long I can deal with this situation. Seeing Cici, pretending she's with Liam." He shook his head. "I hate it."

Connor stared at him. "You're in love with her."

"No I'm not. It's too soon. Besides, I… Oh, shit."

"What?"

"I'm in love with Cici."

Connor grinned. "Well, well, he's finally taken the fall. What took you so long?"

"You know what. Or rather, who."

"I do?"

"Beth. Beth Harrison."

"Good God, Logan, that was years ago. She's the reason you haven't gotten involved with anyone since?"

"She made me doubt my ability to tell if someone is really who I think they are, or they're just snowing me. And then what Caroline did to Liam didn't help."

"So you don't have that problem with Cici?"

"No. I think she's a straight shooter."

"Hmm. Guess who just walked in?"

Logan didn't need to look to know it was Cici. Nevertheless, he did. Damn, he was already tired of the secrecy and it had only been a matter of days since he'd been with her. Looking at her now just made it that much harder. Whenever he saw her he wanted to spirit her off to a private place and steep himself in her.

And that was so not happening.

CICI WAS FINALLY starting to feel like Marietta was home. Or at least that it could become home. As a writer she was something of a loner, which wasn't helped by the fact that she lived on a ranch and not in town, and until she walked into the library, she hadn't met a lot of people beyond Liam, his family and a few neighbors. But thanks to Letty she'd met several people. Since she now owned a car she could go into town anytime she wanted and that also helped immensely.

She looked around for Letty, who hadn't made it yet. No Letty, but she saw Logan and Connor, and they saw her. She was going to have to get used to seeing Logan and acting as if there was nothing between them. She had a cowardly urge to run the other way but Connor was waving at her, and Logan was staring at her so she had no choice but to go to their table.

"Hi, guys."

"Hi, Cici. Are you meeting Liam?"

"No, I'm meeting Letty North but she's not here yet."

"Have a seat and wait for her," Logan said, speaking for the first time. He stood and pulled out the chair for her.

"Thanks." She tried not to look at Logan. All that did was make her think about being with him and want to be with him again. Connor had a shit-eating grin on his face, which made her want to kick him, but she had to content herself with glaring at him.

They talked a little but she and Logan mostly looked at each other until Connor kicked Logan.

"Damn, Connor, why did you kick me?"

"Unless you want everyone in Grey's to know you and Cici are together you need to quit looking at her like she's the icing on your cake and you want to lick her."

"That's not what I'm doing."

Connor merely raised an eyebrow. Cici realized she'd probably been looking at Logan the same way. Luckily, she saw Letty come in just then. She got up and said, "I have to go. My friend is here." She waved at Letty and slid into a booth that was nowhere near Logan and Connor. Except she could still see Logan. She was hopeless.

"Sorry I'm late," Letty said. "Wasn't that Logan and Connor you were with?"

"Yes. I was just passing time until you got here."

"You know, all the McFarland brothers are ridiculously good-looking. But of course you know that seeing as how you're practically engaged to Liam and see his brothers all the time."

"We're nowhere near practically engaged."

The waitress came and took their order.

"I'm starving," Cici said. "I'm going to have a burger and fries. And white wine."

Letty said, "I want the same thing. Except I want a light beer."

She knew she should have chosen a healthier option but at the moment she didn't care.

"Are you and Liam having problems?" Letty asked after the waitress brought their drinks.

Cici knew Letty pretty well by now. It wasn't as if she didn't trust her, but she didn't think she should tell her the truth. At least not all of it.

"You have a terrible poker face, Cici. What's going on?"

"I'm not sure that Liam and I are going to work out."

"Why? He seems like he's such a sweetheart."

"He is. But I'm not sure we're really suited to each other. I don't think he thinks we are either."

"Is that why you've been staring at Logan and Connor the whole time I've been here? Are you interested in Logan? Or is it Connor?"

Damn. She forced a laugh. "Neither one."

Letty looked at her skeptically but didn't call her on the

obvious fib. "If you say so."

Thank God her friend let the subject drop after that. But Cici was going to have to work harder not to let her true feelings show.

Chapter Thirteen

LOGAN WONDERED WHAT he'd done to be cursed. When he and Cici agreed to wait to be together, he hadn't realized how hard it would be to keep his hands off her. There was no possible way he could stop thinking about her. While he didn't live at the ranch anymore he saw Cici at the hospital when she volunteered. He saw her at Grey's when he stopped for a beer or a bite to eat. He saw her at the drugstore. Hell, he saw her all over town. And, of course, he saw her every time he went out to the ranch.

Liam was having enough problems getting help that Logan knew he couldn't bail on him. So he and Connor went out there whenever their schedules allowed—minus some time to sleep.

Every time he saw Cici he wanted her more. He remembered how happy and satisfied she'd looked after they made love. How soft her skin was. When he started remembering how gorgeous she was naked he had to cut himself off. It was a little scary to him how completely she'd bewitched him. She didn't even have to do anything. He simply had to look at her or think about her.

God, who'd have thought he'd fall this hard for a woman? He'd had relationships before. Most had been casual, but not all by any means. But nothing had ever made him feel like he did when he was with Cici.

He tried to analyze why he felt so strongly about her. She was smart but he'd been with other smart women. The way her mind worked was fascinating to him because it was so different from his. Maybe it was the writer in her that made her look at life in an unexpected way. And he was certain it was the writer in her that made her go off into another world. Sometimes in the middle of a discussion. Which, truthfully, could be annoying. And sometimes hilarious. But it was one of those things he'd learned to accept.

For instance, he came over one time and after a long delay Cici answered the door. But instead of inviting him in she simply stared at him. Eventually he had to ask if he could come in. She explained it by saying her head was in a book. More than once he'd asked her a question and if she answered at all, it was a totally off-the-wall comment. Again, her head was in a book.

He still had a hard time believing that Cici wanted him and not Liam. His brother was one of the best people he knew. Maybe Liam and Cici didn't have a lot in common but then, neither did he and Cici. And then there was Liam. How in the hell had Liam not fallen in love with Cici?

Logan had a disturbing thought. Maybe Liam had. But he'd stepped aside when he found out Cici had feelings for

Logan. That would be just like Liam to sacrifice what he wanted so that Cici and Logan could be together. Even if Liam felt that way he'd deny it. He'd already denied having anything more than brotherly feelings for Cici. Logan just had to hope he was telling the truth. The last thing he wanted was to cause Liam more pain.

But giving up Cici wasn't an option either. Cici had been as definite as Liam had been that all she felt for Liam was friendship.

LOGAN KNEW SOMETHING was going on. Maureen wanted everyone to come to dinner at the ranch. Which was difficult given that both Logan and Connor were in medicine and worked strange hours and Liam seemed to be working all the time.

But for their mother they all rearranged work, called in favors, and did whatever they needed to make her happy. Logan didn't mind. He'd get to see Cici, but he knew looking and not touching was going to be hard. So far, every time he'd seen her, aside from that one day when he'd found out the truth about Liam and Cici, and he and Cici had made love, had been a combination of pain and pleasure.

Tonight was the night of the dinner. Clint was coming, along with his married daughter and her husband. According to Liam, Velma and Maureen had been planning for a week.

He said whenever he was around they immediately changed the subject of whatever they were talking about. Obviously, something big was up.

Velma and his mother had gone all out for dinner. Velma had made roast beef, Clint's favorite, he knew. All sorts of side dishes had been prepared. A bevy of desserts were waiting in the kitchen. Dinner was a noisy affair with everyone talking, seated around the large custom-made oak dining room table. After dessert Clint rose and tapped on his beer bottle. Clint was a big man with piercing blue eyes set in a no-nonsense face. In boots and jeans, with his weathered face and shock of shaggy gray hair, he was the quintessential rancher.

"Maureen and I have an announcement. As you all know, Maureen and I have been friends for a long time now. And I've been in love with her for a long time too. So a few weeks ago I asked her to marry me and well, she's finally agreed." He held out his hand, and a smiling Maureen went to his side and took his hand. There was clapping, talking, and a few whistles before Maureen was able to get them to calm down.

"We haven't set a date yet. There are still a few things we need to get sorted out. We thought we'd have it at Clint's house. But first—" She looked at Liam, then Cici. "I think the two of you need to tell us your plans."

Liam and Cici exchanged glances but neither looked at Logan. He knew Liam wasn't ready to tell their mother that he and Cici weren't an item.

"We're still getting to know each other, Mom. We haven't made any plans yet."

"But you shouldn't let us stop *you* from getting married," Cici said.

"I can't leave until Liam has more help. I know you found a full-time hand, but I don't know how he's working out. And what about a ranch manager? Have you had any luck there? Didn't you interview someone recently?"

Liam frowned. "That didn't work out, but I'm still looking. But like Cici said, that shouldn't stop you from marrying Clint."

"We'll talk about it later." And that was all she'd say.

Later, Logan took his brothers aside. "I think Connor is right. I think there's more to her not wanting to marry Clint than leaving Liam without help. Or a wife."

"Then why would she announce that she accepted Clint's proposal?" Liam asked.

"To force your hand," Connor said. "I noticed Clint didn't look real happy when she wouldn't promise a date. He's probably sick of Mom not making up her mind."

"If I were him, I would be," Liam said.

"We need to talk to her and find out what's really going on," Logan said. For their mother's sake but also because the sooner Maureen was taken care of the sooner Cici and Liam could drop their pretend relationship.

After the company left, Logan, Connor, and Liam cornered their mother. Cici went up to bed so they could talk to her alone.

"What is it, boys?"

They looked at Liam, having decided he should be the one to bring it up. "Why are you stalling, Mom?"

"Stalling?"

"About marrying Clint."

"Why are you stalling about marrying Cici?" she countered immediately.

"This isn't about me. It's about you. Besides, Cici and I haven't known each other that long."

"On the other hand," Logan said, "you've had plenty of time and you know Clint really well. He's loved you for years and he's been waiting weeks for you to answer his proposal. Now you've said yes but you won't commit to a date."

"So why are you stalling?" Connor added.

"I'm not. I told you we were getting married."

"Until you heard Liam and Cici say they weren't ready and then you put it off again," Logan said. "And don't act like you didn't. We saw Clint's face. You'd better watch it or Clint will get sick of waiting for you to make up your mind."

"Clint understands."

"He understands why you've been blowing him off?" Connor asked. "I wish I did."

Maureen stood and set her hands on her hips. "I'm not blowing him off. I'm a grown woman and I don't need my sons trying to run my life. I'll get married when and if I decide to. You three need to mind your own business."

"You are our business, Mom," Liam said.

She walked away and they heard her bedroom door slam.

Connor shook his head. "What now?"

"Am I gonna have to get married? I don't think Cici would be down with that."

"I sure as hell am not." Things were already bad enough. The last thing he needed was for Cici to actually marry Liam. "Hire some help, damn it."

"I have. I just can't find a manager. Maybe I'll hire another crook. How about that?"

Logan ignored that. He was frustrated too. "Does Riley have any ideas?"

"No. Why would he? The Fletchers have had the same manager for years."

True. "Seems like you should at least be able to hire some more regular help."

"I did, remember? And yeah, I need another full-time hand. Most people are already working somewhere. That's the problem. The good ones already have jobs."

He finally asked him the question he'd been avoiding for fear of pissing off his brother or making him feel bad. "Is it the money? Because you know I'm good for it. I've lived on the ranch a long time and never felt like I pitched in enough."

"I don't need your damn money," Liam said, clearly annoyed.

No point in pushing him. Liam wouldn't take his money. "Connor and I will see what we can find out. You keep looking and try Riley again."

"Riley has his own set of problems. He doesn't need to be trying to find help for me."

"I don't know, Liam," Logan said. "It looks like you're going to have to let Mom do what she's gonna do. But this isn't all about her, is it? It's about you wanting to settle down." It was about Liam being lonely, in Logan's opinion. "I think you're making a mistake ruling out every woman in Marietta. I'm sure most of them don't give a shit about Caroline."

"It's not about her," Liam said.

"Then what is it about?" Connor asked.

"You two need to mind your own damn business," Liam said, and walked out.

"I don't know why he has such a hard-on about not wanting to date anyone from around here," Logan said to Connor. "If it's not about being jilted then what's it about?"

"Beats the hell out of me," Connor said. "But he sounded pretty definite about us butting out."

He did. But Liam was his brother and Logan felt at least partially responsible for Liam and Cici not working out. Both of them said they'd decided they wouldn't work long before Logan was in the picture. But he couldn't help wondering what would have happened if he hadn't been around. Would Cici have fallen for Liam given a little more time?

Chapter Fourteen

CICI'S PHONE RANG. When she saw the caller ID her stomach sank. It was the prison where her mother was incarcerated. She hadn't talked to her mother since shortly after her trial and imprisonment. Other than that one time, once Cici turned in her parents her mother hadn't spoken to her again. She'd talked to her father a couple of times and visited him once but although he swore he didn't hate her she knew he had mixed emotions. She highly doubted she'd been forgiven. Her mother in particular could hold a grudge forever and helping to send the two of them to prison was the ultimate betrayal.

It hadn't been easy for her to do it. But when her friend Fran had come to her with her suspicions and Cici had investigated she'd realized that her parents were indeed running a scam. But when she confronted them with proof of their crime and demanded they stop and return the money they'd scammed from innocent people, they'd laughed at her. She'd even threatened to go to the cops, but they hadn't believed she'd do it.

Cici had been on her own for a number of years by the

time all that took place, but she knew she was likely to be blamed along with her parents. Fortunately, the SEC, the agency investigating the crime, believed her and found no connection between Cici and the crime. Because of that and in part because she blew the whistle on her parents, she was never charged.

Even so, her life in Fort Worth became unbearable. Everyone knew about her parents' Ponzi scheme and everyone had an opinion. Far too many thought she'd been involved and had gotten off by making a deal. Sometimes she wondered if she'd known what would happen to her life, would she have turned in her parents? But she knew she would have. She couldn't have borne the guilt of knowing what they were doing to innocent people and doing nothing to stop them. Bad enough it had taken her so long to realize what they were doing.

Why was her mother calling her? Her mom had asked to see her after the trial. Cici had gone and regretted it. She could never forget her mother's accusations and fury. She'd ended their conversation saying she never wanted to see her daughter again. Her father had been angry as well. He hadn't understood how she could have turned them in. But as opposed to her mother, he said he still loved her. Would always love her no matter what she'd done. All that flashed through her mind as the phone rang. She picked it up and accepted the collect call. "Mom? Why are you calling? Is something wrong?" Unlike her father, who was in the state penitentiary in Huntsville, her mother had been remanded to a minimum-security prison for white-collar criminals. It wasn't a country club, but it was a hell of a lot better than the state pen.

Her mother laughed harshly. "Is something wrong? Are you for real? I'm in goddamn prison." Cici didn't respond and her mother continued. "Your father is dead and it's all your fault. He was murdered."

Her stomach roiled. "Dad is dead? Oh, my God. What happened? How did he—"

"How did he die? He was shanked in the prison showers. Where he wouldn't have been if you hadn't betrayed your own flesh and blood."

Like she hadn't heard that before. But…her father was dead. "Do they know who did it?"

"If they do, they haven't told me. Besides, what difference does it make? Dead is dead."

Dead. Her father was dead. If it hadn't been for her, if she hadn't turned in her parents, he would still be alive. No matter that what she'd done had been the right thing to do, the guilt was crushing. "Can we—can I claim him? So we can have…a funeral?"

"I sure as hell can't. I'm sure you don't want to be bothered. You can let the prison take care of him."

"No. I'll take care of…him. Is there—"

Apparently, her mother had nothing more to say to her because she hung up while Cici was speaking.

Her father. Dead. Murdered. Her mother was right. It was at least partially her fault. Her parents, both of them, had been decent parents while she was growing up. They'd started becoming more self-absorbed by the end of high school, but they didn't start their criminal career until after Cici left home. They got a taste of having money and their crimes grew from there. Cici always wondered if the idea for the scheme had come from her mother, and she had talked her father into it. Even if she had it didn't make him any less guilty.

She'd tried to help them go straight but they'd refused. And she couldn't ignore her conscience and allow them to continue swindling people. So even now, even with her father dying in a prison murder, she'd done the only thing she could do and live with herself.

Instead she had to live with the guilt of being in part responsible for her father's death.

AFTER SHE MANAGED to compose herself enough to stop crying, she searched out Liam. He was, naturally, with the horses. This time in the round pen. She climbed up on the fence and watched him for a bit, working one of his new horses, a chestnut mare named Heidi.

Liam was the quintessential cowboy in jeans, short-sleeved baby-blue T-shirt that stretched tight across his chest and biceps, boots, and cowboy hat. She wondered again why she'd fallen for Logan when Liam should have been everything she was looking for. It was for the best, though, since Liam hadn't fallen for her either.

"Hey," he said when he saw her. "Did you need something?"

"Yes. To talk to you."

He came over to the fence, leading Heidi. "You look upset. What's wrong?"

"My father died. I have to go home to arrange for the funeral." She didn't tell him her father had been murdered. Or that it had happened while he'd been in prison. That would open up a whole new can of worms.

"Damn, Cici. I'm sorry. Do you want me to come with you?" He looped Heidi's reins over the top rail and took her hand.

"No." She shouldn't have been surprised. The offer was typical Liam. "That's sweet of you to offer but you can't be away from the ranch that long. I don't know how long it will take for me to arrange everything." First she had to call the prison and arrange to have his body shipped to a funeral home. Since her mother was in prison, she hoped they would let her handle things.

"Was it expected?"

"No. It was…sudden."

"That's rough. How's your mom holding up?"

"Not…well." To say the least. Again, she didn't want to

tell him her mother was also in prison and mad as hell. At Cici.

"What about you? How are you?"

"I think I'm still in shock."

"Understandable. Come here," he said and tugged on her hand. "You look like you need a hug."

She really did. She climbed down and put her arms around his waist. He put his arms around her and hugged her. That's all it took to start the tears again. Liam didn't speak, he simply held her and let her cry. She knew it was pointless but once started she couldn't stop.

Cici cried for what she'd lost. For the parents of her childhood. For the people they once were. Decent. Law-abiding. Not criminals out for money regardless of who they hurt. She didn't know why they'd changed, but she suspected one or both had been in debt. Gambling debts, probably. Major debt they had no way of covering. And once they succeeded in covering their debt, once they realized how easy it was to bilk people out of their money, they couldn't stop. No, they could have but they didn't *want* to stop.

Liam patted her back. She could feel the sympathy emanating from him. She sucked in a breath and managed to stop crying, at least for now. She looked up at him. "I've soaked your shirt."

"It'll dry."

"You're a good friend, Liam."

He smiled. "That's me. Everybody's friend." He kissed

her lightly. A kiss of comfort. Of friendship.

WHAT THE BLOODY *hell?* Not only was Cici standing in Liam's arms, but the bastard had just kissed her. So much for his brother's claim to feel nothing more than friendship for Cici. Liam had wanted her all along.

Liam looked up and saw him, then said something to Cici. She turned and looked at him, her face streaked with tears.

"What's wrong? Are you hurt?"

Cici shook her head, but her tears continued to fall and she didn't speak.

"Cici's father died," Liam said, releasing her.

Logan wanted to go to her. He wanted to be the one comforting her. But he couldn't. He had to sit back and let Liam do it. "I'm so sorry, Cici. Is there anything I can do?"

She shook her head again. "I have to—I can't—" She let herself out through the gate and almost ran to the barn. Logan entered the pen as she left.

"What the hell was that?" Logan asked Liam.

"What was what?"

"You kissed her. I saw you."

"Oh, that. It was nothing. She was upset about her father."

"Right. So you were just comforting her."

Liam laughed. "You're jealous. I hate to remind you, but we had every chance to be together if we'd wanted to."

Logan's brows drew together. "Cici said you didn't sleep together."

"You are unbelievable. The woman just lost her father and here you are acting like a jealous fool."

"Do I have reason to be jealous? Wishing you hadn't let her go, Liam?"

"What if I was? She came here to meet me."

"You son of a bitch. I should beat the crap out of you."

"You can try. You want to fight? Come on, then."

Logan knew his only chance was a surprise attack. He started to walk away, turned and threw a punch. But Liam knew his moves and had been ready for him. He easily dodged the punch.

"You're slowing down," Liam said. "That soft living's getting to you."

Logan ignored him, circling him, looking for a break. Heidi neighed and Liam's attention went to the horse. Logan put a fist in his gut.

"Shit." Liam landed a right uppercut to Logan's jaw.

"Stop it! Stop it right now! What do you think you're doing?"

At the sound of Cici's voice they both turned.

"Nothing," Liam said.

"You hit him."

"He hit me first."

She parked her hands on her hips and glared at them. "Why are you fighting?"

"You want to tell her, or should I?" Liam asked him.

Logan shrugged. "He kissed you."

"I'm aware. So what?"

Logan ground his teeth. "No one was around. It wasn't for show."

Cici stared at him with her mouth open. "Are you kidding me? I just found out my father is dead, Logan. Liam was comforting me. Which is a hell of a lot more than you're doing right now."

The fact that she was right did not help at all. Hell, he'd lost his own father. He knew how that felt. "I'm sorry. I was being an ass."

"You got that right."

Man, she didn't pull any punches.

"And as for you," she said to Liam, "'he hit me first' is not a good reason to fight."

"You don't have any brothers, do you?" Liam asked.

"I'm an only child. I told you that."

"Figures. Just fyi, brothers fight."

She ignored that. "I'm going to pack and get to the airport. I'm taking the first plane out of here."

"I can take you," Logan offered.

"I'm taking her," Liam said.

"I can take my car."

"There's no reason to pay to have it sit at the airport

when I can take you."

"Okay. Thank you, Liam. I won't be long." She walked away without saying anything else to Logan.

"Shit. She's pissed at me."

"Do you blame her? Dumbass."

"I was surprised. I thought—I thought you were making a move on her."

"You know we're just friends. Did that really look like some kind of move? Because it wasn't."

"I couldn't help it." Hell, he hadn't realized just how much he loved her until he saw her in Liam's arms and thought about losing her. "I'm in love with her."

"Duh. You're just now figuring that out?"

"I've known for a while, but if you'll remember, I spent a lot of time denying my feelings because I thought you and Cici were together."

Liam had no comment to add to that.

Chapter Fifteen

CICI WISHED SHE could say that returning to Fort Worth hadn't been as bad as she feared, but she couldn't. Maybe it was partly her imagination, but she heard the whispers when people recognized her. The only good thing was seeing her friend Roxanne. Her best friend knew what had happened and believed Cici had nothing to do with it. She'd stood by her, and Cici knew she always would.

Roxanne picked her up at the airport and insisted Cici stay with her. And since she'd sublet her apartment she agreed happily. Roxanne worked from home for a graphic design company. She and Cici had met at college and became friends after discovering they were both from Fort Worth, though they'd gone to different high schools. They'd grown closer over the years, especially after the Ponzi scheme debacle. Roxanne was one of the few friends who'd stuck by her. The only other person who believed in her innocence was Fran, the friend who'd alerted her about the scam in the first place. But Fran had moved out of state and Cici rarely saw her.

Before she left Marietta, Cici had been able to talk to the

warden at the prison and arrange for her father's body to be shipped to a funeral home in Fort Worth. It had arrived earlier that day. Roxanne was going with her to make the final arrangements.

"Are you going to see him?" Roxanne asked her on the way to the funeral home.

"No. I'd rather try to remember him before everything happened. He was a good father when I was young. I...I loved him."

"And you still do. It's okay to still love him, Cici. It doesn't mean you condone what he did."

No, she didn't condone it. But she wondered what had happened to her parents. They hadn't always been like they were now. Or in her father's case, like he was before he'd been killed. Greedy. Manipulative. But beneath that there was still a core of the sweet man she'd known as a child. The man who'd told her he'd always love her. Even after she'd turned him in.

With Roxanne's support she arranged for the cremation, and the burial of his ashes in the plot her parents had reserved would take place two days later. She waited until they returned to Roxanne's house to call her mother. Given her mother's reaction when she called to tell Cici of her father's death, she dreaded this conversation.

It went pretty much as she'd expected. Her mother barely stopped berating her long enough for Cici to tell her about the arrangements. Cici had talked to the warden and learned that since her mother was in a minimum-security facility, Cici would be allowed to pick her up and return her after the service with no prison official accompanying her.

She hung up feeling totally drained. Roxanne shot her a worried glance as they drove to her house. "I wish there was something I could do."

"You're doing it. I can't tell you how much I appreciate what you've done and are doing for me. I feel guilty for involving you in all this."

"Don't be silly. You'd do the same for me if I needed you." She sent Cici a worried glance. "Have you talked to Logan since you got here?"

When they'd video-chatted while she was in Marietta she'd told Roxanne what was really going on with Liam and Logan and her. "Yes, but not since yesterday. I'm sure he's working."

Later that evening her phone rang. "It's Liam," she said to Roxanne, a little surprised.

"Hey," he said when she answered. "How's it going?"

"About like I expected. The service is in a couple of days. I'll come back the day after."

"Are you sure you don't need me to come down there?"

"No, my friend Roxanne is helping me. But I really appreciate the offer."

"Call me if you need me."

"He is such a nice man," she said when the call ended.

"But you're not in love with him," Roxanne said. "Is he

in love with you?"

"Liam? No. We're friends. That's all."

"Are you sure that's all it is for him?"

Was she sure? She hoped so. She didn't want to do anything to hurt Liam. "We decided we were better as friends before I ever told him about my feelings for Logan." In fact, she hadn't told Liam about her feelings for his brother until a good while later.

Not long after that Logan called. "Sorry I didn't call earlier but I've been swamped at work. How are you?"

"I'm okay. The service is day after tomorrow. I'm kind of dreading seeing my mom."

"Still not getting along?"

She'd told Logan that she wasn't close to either parent. "You could say that." In fact, she'd say her mother hated her. Even though her dad had been angry with her, especially at first, she knew he didn't hate her. Cici told Logan her plans, and that she'd be back day after tomorrow.

"I wish I could be there for you. It must be so hard going through it by yourself."

"Roxanne is with me so I'm not alone. But thank you. It helps knowing you get it." Of course, his dad hadn't been a felon like hers was, but he knew what it was like to lose a parent.

"I want to see you," he said. "I want to be with you."

"I want that too, but we decided we wouldn't be together while I'm still technically with Liam."

"I know, but I hate not being with you."

"Me too. But I don't see a way around it."

They talked a little more before Logan got paged and had to go. She knew she should tell him about her past. But not now when they weren't even dating publicly. If they were ever able to be open about their relationship, she would.

But she dreaded telling him. Her story and her parents' story in all the sordid details. What would he think? Surely he wouldn't believe she had anything to do with the scam. He couldn't think that of her.

Could he?

"CICI'S GETTING BACK tonight," Liam said when Logan answered the phone.

"I know. She told me."

"Can you pick her up?"

"I figured you'd do it."

"I can't. Can you help me out?"

Like he minded. "All right. Give me the flight information."

Liam told him. "Thanks, Logan."

"Believe me, it's no hardship." After the first couple of days when he'd been swamped at work he'd talked to Cici or video-chatted with her daily. He knew she was sad about her father and torn about her mother but she hadn't wanted to talk about any of it. It seemed to him she just wanted to forget it as quickly as possible. He knew from personal experience that wasn't going to work but he didn't think she'd appreciate him telling her that.

Her plane was late. So far over an hour late, for a flight that had started out almost a red-eye. Hardly worth going back to Marietta tonight. They could stay in Bozeman. He could be alone with Cici. And he didn't need to go in to work until noon. He couldn't have planned it better if he'd tried.

When he finally saw her his heart squeezed a little. Who'd have ever thought he'd be this gone over a woman? Not him. He liked women. He liked sex. But other than with Beth years ago, he'd never felt the urge to settle down with one woman. He'd been too wrapped up in his career. He still was but now he could see himself adding Cici into the mix. Which was crazy. They couldn't even be together in public in Marietta yet.

She wore a red long-sleeved dress with tiny flowers, a V-neck, and a waist that cinched in to show her figure. On her feet she wore red heels that tied around her ankles and had a wedge heel. She looked young and summery. Her thick, dark hair was down, flowing over her shoulders and back. Her brown eyes sparkled when she saw him. "Hi, Logan. I thought Liam was picking me up."

"He asked me to. Do you have more luggage?"

"Yes, I got some things out of storage in Fort Worth. When I moved into my apartment there I had to store some things thinking I'd get a house and need them but I never did." She shrugged. "I'm glad I didn't now. Sorry I'm so late. They changed our gate about twelve times, delayed take-off time, and when we finally got on the plane, it sat on the runway forever before we wound up changing planes. Mechanical problems."

"No problem. How are you?" he asked as they walked to the baggage claim.

"I'm okay, considering. It's been stressful to say the least. My mother is difficult at the best of times, so of course now that my dad is gone she's even worse."

"I'm sorry. Is there anything I can do? Do you want to talk about it?"

Her voice was shaky when she answered. "No. I want to forget it. I think I'm emotionally overloaded."

He could imagine she was. "I'm here if you decide you need to talk."

"Thanks. Look, there's one of my bags."

After picking up her luggage Logan said, "It's awfully late. What do you say we stay tonight in Bozeman?"

Their gazes met and held. She smiled. "That sounds like a plan. Should we let Liam know we're staying?"

"I'll give him a call."

Forty-five minutes later they checked into a nearby hotel. They'd stopped and picked up fast food, which they'd both scarfed down. Logan had called Liam and told him they wouldn't be back until the following day.

Cici went into the bathroom when they got to the room. She'd taken her backpack in with her. A short while later she came out with her hair brushed and gestured for him to take the bathroom. Since he hadn't expected to stay overnight he'd picked up a toothbrush and toothpaste, along with other necessities at the airport. He came out to find Cici looking out the window.

He went to her and put his arms around her. She sighed and leaned back against him. "Logan? Do you have protection?"

He smiled and went back in the bathroom, tossing a box of condoms on the bedside table when he came out. "Bought them when your plane was so late. Hoping to stay overnight."

"Good." She sighed. "You're going to think I'm silly."

"Why?"

"I'm nervous."

"Why are you nervous?" Logan asked.

He sure as hell wasn't. He'd been dreaming about this ever since the last time they'd made love. But he'd had no idea when, and sometimes if, the dream would become a reality.

"We don't know each other that well. What if we're making a mistake? What if this is just a fleeting attraction?"

"Are you regretting not being with Liam?" He held his

breath for her answer. If she said yes it would kill him.

"No. I care about Liam but not like that."

"I can't speak for you, obviously, but for me this isn't a fleeting attraction. To me it's a lot more. I've fallen for you, Cici."

She turned in his arms and looked up at him. Her eyes, a deep chocolate brown, glistened. "Oh, Logan. I've fallen for you too." She put her arms around his neck and kissed him.

"You can't imagine how many times I've thought about being with you like this," Logan said. He kissed her, pulling her closer until her breasts were smashed against his chest. Deepening the kiss, he grabbed the skirt of her dress and slowly drew it up, then ran his hands over her gorgeous ass, clad only in tiny panties. She wrapped her legs around his waist and he walked them toward the bed. He let her down slowly, both of them groaning as she slid down his body. She turned her back to him, pulling her hair over her shoulder to expose her neck.

"Will you unzip me?"

"Gladly." He unzipped her, then pushed the dress off her shoulders. It fell to the floor, pooling at her feet. Turning her around, he looked at her pretty, lacy white bra. Her nipples were already beaded. He bent and licked one through the fabric, drew it into his mouth and sucked. She groaned, her arms tightening around him.

He unfastened her bra and she flung it away, leaving her dressed only in a tiny pair of red panties and her sandals. She sat on the bed and propped her foot on his leg, dangerously close to his hard-on.

"Untie me?" Her voice was whiskey-smooth, laced with desire.

"That sounded really wicked." But he untied that shoe and slipped it off before moving to the other one.

She laughed. "I meant it to. But here I am, practically naked and you still have on all your clothes. Shouldn't we remedy that?"

He'd kicked off his shoes and taken off his socks earlier. He yanked his T-shirt over his head, unbuckled his belt, unbuttoned and unzipped his jeans, sliding them down and off along with his boxers. Cici watched him, desire lighting her eyes.

"You are so beautiful." Her breasts were high, medium-sized, the perfect size for his hands. Her body was a dream, her skin smooth and tempting. He sat on the edge of the bed and pulled her close, urging her to sit on his lap. She straddled him, the silk of her panties the only thing between them, his cock growing even harder. Hands on her hips, he kissed her, shuddering when she stroked herself up and down, her sex against his.

He kissed his way down her chest. She leaned back, her breasts thrusting upward, her nipples tight and teasing. He took one in his mouth, sucking on it until she writhed, then moved to the other one.

"I want you inside me," she said. She stood and pushed

her panties down her legs as he grabbed a condom and rolled it down over his aching cock. Then he helped her straddle him again, his cock at her entrance, and she sank down on him inch by inch. Their gazes met and held and they both groaned.

Her body gloved him, he thrust up as she came down, faster and faster until she cried out and he felt her pulsing, tightening around him until, with a searing burst of pleasure, he came.

It took him a while to move. Cici had collapsed against him and it felt so good to just hold her he didn't want to spoil the moment.

They slept in each other's arms, waking more than once to make love. In the morning Logan woke first and watched Cici sleep. She opened her eyes and smiled at him. "What's wrong?" she asked. "Am I drooling?"

He laughed and kissed her. "Nope. No drool." He'd never watched a woman sleep before. But she looked so sweet and peaceful. He wished they could stay there, in their own little world, forever.

"I hate to go back," he said, holding her, the feeling of peace fading. "Who knows when we'll be able to be together again?"

"I know. I hate it too. But we don't have to leave right this minute, do we?"

He glanced at the clock. "As long as I can be at the hospital by one I'm good."

"In that case," she said, and rolled on top of him. "I want you, Logan." Her voice was husky, inviting. Who was he to argue with a beautiful, naked woman?

He shoved his hands in her hair and kissed her and soon thinking was impossible as he steeped himself in her.

Chapter Sixteen

A FEW DAYS after returning from her trip to Fort Worth, Cici met Letty at Grey's for lunch. She'd volunteered at the hospital that morning so it was easy to meet for lunch in town. When she walked into the restaurant it took her a moment for her eyes to adjust. Once they did she saw Letty standing at the bar talking to a pretty woman with a long blond braid, wearing jeans, boots, and a baby-blue T-shirt that read: *I like horses, dogs, and maybe four people.*

"Hi, Cici," Letty said. "This is Val Fletcher. Val, this is Cici Bradley. Val is Riley's sister. You know, they live on the ranch neighboring the McFarlands'."

"Hi, Val. It's nice to meet you." Although she'd met Riley, he was the only one of his family she'd met so far. It was nice to meet another woman. Through Letty mostly, she'd met a number of other people, but Letty was still her only close friend in Marietta. She started to offer her hand but Val had stuck hers in her back pocket.

"You're the one Liam met over the internet."

"That's right."

Val looked her up and down with a decidedly unfriendly

expression but didn't speak. *She looks like she'd just as soon skewer me as talk to me.* Cici couldn't imagine why.

"Why don't you join us for lunch?" Letty asked.

Val shook her head. "Thanks, but I've got to go. It was good seeing you, Letty." She nodded at Cici and left.

"Wow," Cici said watching her leave. "I don't think I'm one of the four people she likes. Is she always that unfriendly?"

Letty looked puzzled for a moment. "No, she's usually really friendly. That was weird."

They took a seat at one of the booths. "I'd ask if I did something to offend her, but we've never even met until now."

Letty slapped a hand to her head. "Oh, I know what it is. I can't believe it didn't occur to me. Val has a crush on Liam. Has had one for years."

"Years? She looks awfully young."

"She's twenty-three. Old enough."

"Does Liam know how she feels?"

"According to Val, Liam is completely oblivious. In fact, she told me she didn't think Liam even sees her as a woman."

"She's very pretty. And obviously a cowgirl."

"Yes. She works with horses on the Fletcher ranch." Letty sighed and added, "I lived with the Fletchers during my senior year of high school. You know, after my parents died."

"I remember you said that. I'm so sorry."

"Me too. They died suddenly right before I started my senior year. Even though Val is a few years younger than me we were friends. I didn't have any relatives and I wasn't eighteen yet, so rather than me having to go into foster care, the Fletchers took me in."

"I'm sorry for your loss. That must have been so hard."

"It was but the Fletchers did their best to make me feel welcome. I'll never forget what they did for me."

"I'm glad you had them."

"Me too. Val and I are still friends, obviously."

"What about Riley? Are you still friends?"

"Sort of. It's a long story."

"Which you don't want to talk about."

Letty shrugged. The waiter came to take their order and Cici allowed the subject to drop.

"You look like you're plotting something," Letty said after the waiter left.

Cici laughed. "I kind of am."

"What's going on?"

"Val has nothing to fear from me."

"Why? Did you and Liam break up?"

"Not exactly." The waiter brought their drinks and left again. She stirred sugar into her iced tea. "I'll tell you about it once we get our food." No way did she want the truth getting out. At least not until Liam gave her the okay. She trusted Letty could keep her mouth shut. Other people, not so much.

They chatted about Cici's book and Letty's work until their food arrived. Both of them had ordered grilled chicken salad. "All right, spill," Letty said.

"I need to swear you to secrecy before I tell you anything."

Letty rolled her eyes. "Consider me sworn."

"You know I told you I was questioning whether Liam and I were suited to each other." Letty nodded. "We talked about it and Liam and I decided that we were better as friends than anything else."

"If that's true, then why does everyone think you're still together?"

"Because he wants his mother to believe it." She went on to explain the whole situation to her.

"Whoa," Letty said when she finished. "So Liam thinks he needs to be married or, at least, engaged before his mom will leave?"

"Right. I have my doubts that it's going to work, but I feel like it's the least I can do for Liam. After all, he went to a lot of trouble and expense to fly me out here and let me live at his place. And the damn stubborn man won't let me pay him back."

"I wouldn't expect him to. That would go totally against his nature."

"Yeah," she said glumly.

"So you can't date anyone else until Liam's mom moves out. Or he admits it's not working."

"About that…"

"Cici, what are you planning?"

"There's another man. But we've agreed to keep our…relationship secret."

"Who is it?"

"Logan."

Letty's eyes widened. "Logan McFarland, Liam's *brother*? Are you kidding me?"

"No. And before you ask, Logan and I didn't get together until after Liam and I decided we weren't suited."

"Liam knows?"

"Of course Liam knows. Do you really think I'd go behind his back? With his brother?"

"Calm down. Of course I don't think that. But…are you sure he's okay with you and Logan getting together?"

"He says he is. I believe him. He doesn't act like he thinks of me as more than a friend."

"That's good. What's he going to do if he can't convince his mom to get married?"

"I don't know. He's looking for more help but I'm not sure that will pacify his mother. Meanwhile Logan and I can't be together until Liam figures out his plan isn't working."

"Not that it's any of my business—" Letty began.

"Go ahead. Ask it. Have Logan and I slept together?"

"Well, have you?"

"Yes." More than once. Not that Letty needed all the

details. "But we decided we couldn't be together again until we can be open about it. And it's hard. Every time I see him I want to be with him."

Her only consolation was that it wouldn't be forever.

IT WAS GETTING harder and harder for Cici to pretend Logan was nothing more than Liam's brother to her. Judging by some of the heated glances Logan sent her way whenever she saw him, he felt the same. They hadn't been together since their night at the hotel in Bozeman. Hadn't so much as touched, much less kissed. And as far as she could tell, Maureen was in no hurry to marry her rancher and move out.

Cici was in the barn waiting for Liam to go riding with her when Logan walked in. They stared at each other for a moment, then he grabbed her hand, led her into the tack room, and closed the door. He let go of her hand and cupped her face in his hands. "This is driving me crazy." And then he kissed her.

His tongue swept inside her mouth and she met it eagerly with hers. His hands fell to her waist, drawing her closer. She moaned and pressed against him. Wrapped her arms around his neck. Lost herself in the pleasure, in the heat swamping her, firing her blood.

He drew back and said, against the skin of her neck, "If I

don't have you soon I'm going to lose it."

She groaned. "I know." She put her hand in his hair, running her fingers through the soft, silky strands. "I'm going to talk to Liam."

"Good." He took her mouth again in a deep, possessive kiss. "This pretense has gone on long enough." He slipped a hand beneath her T-shirt, cupping her breast, running his thumb over the nipple covered by her lacy bra.

Her breathing quickened as he kissed her again, plucked her nipple, and massaged her breast. It was all she could do not to strip off her clothes and throw herself at him.

"What in the hell is going on?"

They jumped apart. Maureen stood in the doorway. Neither of them had even heard her open the door.

Oh, shit. Shit, shit, shit. Why hadn't they locked the door?

"It's not what it looks like," Logan said.

"Oh, really?" She eyed them both, her eyes sparkling with anger. "I think it's exactly what it looks like. If you can drag yourself away from *your brother's girl*, I'd like to talk to you." With that she left, slamming the door shut behind her.

"Oh, God, your mother hates me. She thinks I'm a two-timing, horrible person. She thinks I'm cheating on Liam with you. What are we going to do?"

"Tell her the truth, obviously. What else can we do after she caught us kissing?"

"Not to mention you were feeling me up. Which I'm sure she also saw." She wanted to sink into the floor.

"It could have been worse. At least we were fully dressed."

"Not funny, Logan."

He shrugged. "I'll find Liam and we'll go talk to her."

"He was supposed to go riding with me."

"Maybe he forgot." At the door he turned and looked at her. "One good thing," he said with a smile lifting his mouth. "We won't have to hide anymore."

LOGAN WENT LOOKING for Liam. There was no way he was going to face his mother alone. Especially since this whole secrecy thing was Liam's idea. Not his.

He found him in the loft of the barn, throwing hay down. "Did you forget you were supposed to ride with Cici?"

"Crap. Is it that late?"

"Never mind that. We need to talk."

"I'm busy." He'd gone back to tossing hay.

"It's important."

Liam stopped and looked down at him. "What is it?"

Rather than get a crick in his neck, he climbed up the ladder to the loft. "The secret's out."

"What secret?"

"The fact that you and Cici aren't together, but she and I are."

"What happened?"

He rubbed a hand over the back of his neck. "Mom found Cici and me together."

"Damn, Logan, couldn't you keep it in your pants for a little while longer?"

"For God's sake, we weren't *doing it*." God, he shuddered to think what that would have been like. "We were in the tack room and Mom came in. We were kissing."

"Uh-huh. Kissing like you were about to do it, right?"

"It's not like that." He paced away. He didn't like how Liam was holding the pitchfork.

"Yeah? Then what is it like?"

"I told you, I'm in love with her. It's killing me to see her with you and know we can't be together."

Liam shook his head. "What a clusterfuck."

"We have to tell Mom the truth. We can't wait any longer."

"I don't think my plan is working anyway. I'm not sure anything is going to work short of me actually getting married. Even if I hire more help she won't be satisfied."

Logan thought it hadn't been a great idea in the first place but there was no sense telling Liam that. He obviously felt bad enough.

"Where's Cici?"

"In her room. I told her you and I would deal with Mom. She wanted to come too but I said I thought it would be better with just you and me."

"I guess it had to happen sometime," Liam said.

Once Liam had washed up they walked to the house together. Velma was in the kitchen making dinner. "I don't know what you did," she said when they entered, "but I haven't seen your mother that mad in a long time."

Great. "Is she in her room?" Logan asked.

"Yes. I don't suppose you want to tell me what's going on?"

Liam answered her. "Cici and I aren't really together. She and Logan are."

"I take it Maureen didn't know that."

"No. You don't seem surprised," Logan said.

"I've known you boys since you were in diapers. So no, I'm not surprised. But your mom obviously was."

"She thinks Liam doesn't know about Cici and me."

"I don't envy you two."

"Velma? How did you know?" Logan asked her.

"I saw the way you look at her and the way she looks at you. Besides, it was obvious, to me at least, that Liam wasn't hung up on her. Don't know why Maureen didn't see that."

"You go ahead," Liam said. "I'll be there in a minute."

Logan knocked on his mother's bedroom door. "Mom? Can I come in?"

She didn't answer so he tested the door, relieved to find it unlocked. He walked in, wincing when he saw his mom's face. Mad didn't even come close to describing it. She sat in her 'reading chair' next to the window that looked out over some of the pastures and woods of the ranch.

"Well?" his mother said. Logan started to answer but she wasn't finished. "What is *wrong* with you? How could you—and Cici! I've never been so disappointed in—"

Thank God, Liam walked in just then. Their mother immediately shut her mouth.

"Logan told me what happened."

"He did? You mean he told you—"

"About you walking in on him and Cici. Yeah."

"You don't look upset. Why? What's going on?"

"We haven't been…truthful with you. Cici and I aren't really together. We haven't been for a while now. Logan and she are."

"Then what the hell have you been doing all this time pretending you were interested in Cici?"

Liam sent him a 'help me' look. "He did it for you," Logan said.

"For me? That makes no sense at all."

"We want you to marry Clint, but you keep putting it off," Liam said. "I think you've been worried I'd never get married ever since Caroline jilted me. So I thought if you believed Cici and I were together that you'd finally marry Clint."

"That's the dumbest idea I've ever heard. I do not need my grown sons telling me what to do. Does Connor know about this?"

"He does but he hasn't really had anything to do with it.

We just asked him to keep his mouth shut."

"You and Cici pretended to be together. How long have you been pretending? And how long have Logan and Cici been having an affair? An affair that you condoned, Liam?"

"Cici and I decided we were better as friends a while ago. As for Logan, I'll let him tell you about that."

"Nothing happened between Cici and me until after she and Liam decided to be friends." This really wasn't his mother's business, but he wasn't going to tell her that. He didn't have a death wish. Still doubtful, she looked from one to the other. "Mom, you have to know I wouldn't do that to Liam."

Maureen snorted. "Where is Cici? I'd like to hear this from her."

Logan started to speak but Liam beat him to it. "Cici was only doing what I asked her to. She wanted everything out in the open long ago. This wasn't her idea."

Maureen was quiet for a long time. "I don't understand why you felt it necessary to lie to me. And I don't appreciate it. When and if I marry Clint is my business. But let me ask you this, Liam. How do you think you're going to run this ranch without me? You still haven't hired a ranch manager and you only hired one full-time hand. You're already doing the work of two men. Your brothers have their own jobs, and they can't always be here to help. Not to mention, I'm sure you haven't even asked Velma what are her plans if I move out. So what are you going to do?"

"I have another new hand coming tomorrow. I think he's going to work out. And I've got more interviews set up with ranch managers since the last one was a no-go."

"Good. But that still doesn't solve the problem." When they started to argue she held up a hand. "I've heard enough. You two can go now."

They left her room, closing the door behind them.

"That was fun," Logan said.

"Yeah, about as much as being kicked in the chest by Riptide would be."

"Do you really have a new hand coming? And appointments?"

Liam scowled. "No, but I will by tomorrow."

Chapter Seventeen

CICI COULDN'T SIT still. She wondered how it was going with Maureen. She didn't mind admitting she was worried. Did Maureen hate her? Of course she did. Not only would she think Cici had done Liam wrong, she was bound to think Cici was terrible for Logan.

She dragged out the large suitcase she'd brought back from Fort Worth. Most of her stuff had been put in storage but she'd left some clothes and a few other things—primarily her extra research books and fiction—with Roxanne. She'd shipped the books she needed to the ranch and they'd come in a few days before. Luckily, she hadn't had a chance to open many of the boxes.

Someone knocked on the door. "Come in."

"What are you doing?" Logan asked, obviously seeing her open suitcase on the bed.

"Packing. I can't stay here."

"Why not?" Liam asked, walking in behind his brother. "There's no reason for you to leave. I'm not kicking you out. You don't have another place to stay, do you?"

She'd worried about that until she'd talked to Letty.

"Letty told me that Walker and Calum Quest have an apartment over their film production studio that they rent out to family and friends. She offered to call them and ask if I can stay there until I find an apartment for the long term." Or at least until she figured out what she wanted to do. Her phone rang. "That's Letty's ringtone."

Her friend had offered to share her own apartment with Cici, but she'd told Letty that she'd only do it in an emergency. Letty lived in a tiny one-bedroom apartment and while Cici could stay with her for a night or two she couldn't stay indefinitely. It was barely big enough for Letty.

Both men looked at her as she hung up. They both looked ready to argue but she wasn't having it. "I'm staying at the Quests'. Letty arranged it. Now y'all can go. I need to finish packing."

She'd made up her mind and no argument they presented—and they made a number of them—could change it. Finally she said, "Your mother doesn't want me here."

"She didn't tell you that," Liam said. "In fact, you haven't talked to her, have you?"

"I can't imagine her saying that. If she did I'll talk to her," Logan said.

"No, don't. I don't need to be hit on the head with a baseball bat to know when I'm not wanted. I'm leaving and that's that. I'm not making your mother any more uncomfortable than she already is."

"If you're sure…" Logan began.

"Positive."

"All right. I have to go to work. And I know Liam has a lot to do too. But Connor's off and said he was coming to the ranch. I'm sure he can help you."

"I can move myself. I don't have that much stuff."

"I've got to go," Liam said. "I wish you'd reconsider."

"I appreciate that so much, Liam. But it will be better for everyone if I leave."

Liam nodded and left.

While they were talking Logan had used his phone. "Connor's almost here. He said he'd be glad to help you."

There was no point in arguing with the man, at least about this. "Fine. Don't you need to go?"

"I'm going." He put his hands on her shoulders, drew her closer, and kissed her. "I'll call you later to see how it went."

She had one more thing to do before she left. Something she really didn't want to do but she knew she had to.

She wasn't sure where Maureen was but decided to try her room first. "Come in," Maureen said when she knocked.

"I'm moving into town today and I wanted to thank you for your hospitality and kindness while I was here. And I'm sorry for how things turned out."

"I don't like being lied to. By my sons, by you, by anyone. I have no idea why Liam thought he needed to lie to me but—"

"He wants you to be happy. He thinks you will be if you

marry Clint."

"Whether I marry Clint or not is my business. Not Liam's, or Logan's, or Connor's."

"I'm sorry," Cici said. "I hope you can forgive me one day."

Maureen gave her a measuring look, then smiled. "I probably will. After all, this is more my sons' fault than yours. And…I'm glad you weren't cheating on Liam. That didn't sound like the woman I've come to know."

It wasn't 'you're forgiven' but at least it wasn't get lost and never darken my door again.

CICI LOOKED AROUND the studio apartment with satisfaction. Logan must have told Connor what had happened because he very carefully didn't ask a lot of questions. Thank God he didn't. From what she knew of him he wasn't usually so circumspect.

"Are you sure this is what you want?" Connor asked before he left. "I know Liam wouldn't mind you staying at the ranch."

"But your mother would. And I would be really uncomfortable. Besides, I've already moved, and it's time I was on my own."

"I've got work this afternoon but if you need more help give me a call. There might be nothing going on."

"Thanks, Connor. I really appreciate it."

"No problem." He smiled and left.

The only things she'd really needed help with were the boxes of books. A lot of her research for the books she wrote took place on the internet, and naturally, she had ebooks too, but she loved real books you could hold in your hand. The books—an eclectic mix of fiction, nonfiction, and research in hardback and paperback—were stacked in boxes in a corner of the apartment, where they'd stay until she found a more permanent place. Her laptop sat on the small dining table along with all of her chargers. She could work here. And a good thing since she was behind on her current book and her deadline was drawing near. No surprise, she'd been having a hard time concentrating lately.

There were two apartments built over the Quests' garage turned film production studio. Her apartment was light and airy and surprisingly spacious. Directly over the studio, the front of the apartment, where the kitchen sat, had a small window and faced Bramble Lane. The back had a large picture window in the living area, which overlooked a backyard and quiet street. There was a queen-sized bed with two bedside tables against one wall. Several feet in front of the bed, a small couch and coffee table faced the opposite wall with a TV hanging on it. The kitchen was tiny but serviceable. She sure didn't need a large one since she didn't cook but rather scrounged. And finally, there was a decent-sized bathroom with an apartment-sized, stacked washer and dryer, and a small walk-in closet.

Everything she needed. No distractions so she could get some serious work done. She wouldn't think about the fact that she missed the bustle of the ranch, the dogs and the horses. As soon as she could she was getting a dog. And if she wanted to ride she knew Liam would be fine with that.

She put on her writing music and got to work. Sometime later, she heard a knock on her door and looked up. Surely it wasn't Logan. He should still be at work. Then she glanced at the time and realized she'd worked for several hours straight.

She opened the door and they stared at each other for a long moment. Then he stepped inside, yanked her into his arms and laid a dizzying kiss on her. She threw her arms around his neck and kissed him back.

LOGAN BOOSTED HER up and she wrapped her legs around him. "I've really missed you," he said.

"I've missed you too," she said between kisses. He walked to the bed with her, Cici shedding clothes as they went. When they reached the bed Logan let her down slowly, her body sliding against his in a move designed to make him crazy. After work he'd gone home and changed into jeans and a T-shirt. Cici slid her hands beneath the shirt and pushed it up.

"You're wearing too many clothes," she told him.

"So are you." Her upper body was bare but she still wore her jeans. He yanked his shirt over his head, sat to take off shoes and socks. Then he stood again and started on his jeans, first taking some condoms out of his pocket and tossing them on the bed. At the same time he watched her as she unzipped her own pants and pushed them down her legs. All she wore now was a tiny pair of bikini panties.

"Damn, you really are gorgeous."

"I'm not but I'm glad you think so."

He pushed her back on the bed, landing in the cradle of her legs, the thin wisp of nylon the only barrier between them. "I want you so much, I don't think I can go slow."

"Good. I don't want slow. I want you. Inside me."

He grabbed a condom and covered himself, then skimmed her panties down her legs. He slid a finger inside her and groaned, feeling her so tight and wet. Cici wrapped her legs around him and said huskily, "Now, Logan."

He thrust inside her, both of them groaning. "You feel so good." Like coming home. Like he was exactly where he was supposed to be. He pushed inside her and pulled out in a slow rhythm at first, then faster and faster until he felt her spasm around him and, unable to wait any longer, he came in wave after wave.

He rolled aside and drew her close, realizing that as far as foreplay went, there'd been essentially none. He got up and went to the bathroom, wetting a washcloth and bringing it back to her, then cleaning her up. "Sorry I was so quick."

"That's all right. I wanted quick."

"But I didn't get to appreciate all of you." He got in bed, kissed her slowly, caressed her breast, thumbing her nipple until it stood in a stiff peak. He wrapped his lips around her nipple, sucking it and flicking it with his tongue. Then he moved to the other one.

Cici gasped and put her hands in his hair. "You can't possibly…"

"Not this minute but soon. Now be quiet and let me make love to you."

"When you put it that way…"

They spent the evening together, making love, talking, eating, and making love again. He explored her body leisurely, playing with her breasts, kissing and sucking her nipples until she pushed him onto his back saying, "My turn." And she took her time, kissing and caressing him until he was so hot he wondered if he could wait until he was inside her or he was going to implode right then. She picked up a condom and rolled it down his shaft, so slowly he didn't need to see the wicked smile on her face to know she was teasing him. Then she took him inside her, sinking down, surrounding him with hot, wet paradise. She rode him until she came, calling his name and he followed her over the edge and exploded.

Logan picked up Chinese food takeout from the local restaurant. Since the small dining table was covered with

Cici's computer, books, notebooks, notes, and a printer, they ate on the coffee table in front of the couch. Logan was still adjusting to the fact that they didn't have to hide their relationship anymore. Not that he wasn't happy about it.

"This is really good," Cici told Logan. "I love Chinese food." She picked up one of the fortune cookies and broke it to read the fortune inside. "You will meet a fascinating member of the opposite sex," she read. "That's spot-on," she said with a laugh. "Except I already have. What does yours say?"

Logan broke his cookie and pulled out the small slip of paper. *Trouble is coming*, he read. Damn, he didn't like that. He crumpled the paper and tossed it in the sack with the trash.

"What did it say?" Cici asked. "Why did you throw it away?"

"It was one of those generic ones. Something about traveling." Cici shot him a skeptical glance but didn't say any more. Good God, what was wrong with him? He worried about what a *fortune cookie* said?

Chapter Eighteen

OVER THE NEXT couple of weeks Cici and Logan spent all their spare time together. Cici still felt a little weird going out in public but people were going to have to get used to seeing her and Logan together. No one was rude enough to ask her what she was doing with Logan when everyone in town knew she'd come to Marietta to meet Liam. But she knew they wondered.

Of course, when she said no one was rude enough to ask her she hadn't reckoned with Carol Bingley. Carol, who worked at the pharmacy, asked her specifically what she was doing 'messing around' with Logan when she was supposed to be with Liam. Cici was so dumbfounded she didn't know what to say. When she managed to close her mouth, she told her that she and Liam were just friends. And she did not add, *Not that it's any of your business.*

She told Logan about it that evening.

He laughed. "Carol Bingley is Marietta's resident gossip. She knows everything, or thinks she does. She's harmless. Don't worry about it."

They were going to the Graff for dinner. Not to the fancy restaurant there but to the Irish-themed pub later to meet a couple of Logan's friends, Sean and Honey Gallagher. She knew that Sean was an ER doctor who worked with Logan and Logan had told her that his wife, Honey, was a barrel racer who fairly recently had started teaching kids to barrel race. She'd met Mia Gallagher through Letty, but not any of the others, even though their ranch wasn't all that far from the McFarland ranch.

The couple were already seated in a green leather booth by the time she and Logan got there. They rose and all shook hands. Cici was totally crazy about Logan but she wasn't blind. Sean was a damn good-looking man. Tall, with a broad chest that she bet was nicely muscled, sandy-brown hair and gray eyes, she was certain he made a lot of women's hearts flutter. But judging from the way he looked at Honey, Sean was obviously head over heels about his wife. She was a beautiful woman with black hair and blue eyes, and she was obviously pregnant.

Their server came and took their orders shortly afterward. As often happens with couples, Logan and Sean started talking—about sports, not medicine—leaving Cici and Honey to talk. "The only sport I want to talk about is rodeo but Sean likes almost everything."

"I like baseball," Cici said. "But I can take or leave the others." She changed the subject. "When are you due?"

"Two more months. I can't wait. I feel like a boat."

Cici laughed. "Well, you don't look like one. Logan said

you're teaching barrel racing?"

"Yes, my OB and my husband both vetoed me barrel racing until after the baby is born. So, those who can't do, teach." She laughed. "But I'm enjoying teaching, which shocked me at first."

"I'm sure you'll be back to racing by next season."

"I hope so. Do you ride, Cici?"

"I hadn't in a long time until I came to Marietta. But Liam had me up on a horse the day after I got here."

"Speaking of Liam, I haven't heard of him and Logan trying to kill each other. What's up with that?" She winced as soon as she finished speaking. "Oh, crap. I told Sean I'd try not to ask about things you probably don't want to talk about. Screwed that up, didn't I?"

Cici had to laugh. "No, it's okay. I'm sure a lot of people are wondering about that. In fact, Carol Bingley cornered me the other day to ask me about it." She told her what Carol had said. "I told her Logan and I didn't get together until after Liam and I decided to be just friends. I'm not sure she believed me."

"I believe you. I've known the McFarlands for a while now and Logan doesn't strike me as the type to go after his brother's girl. Not unless Liam was okay with it."

"Thanks. Logan wouldn't do that. And neither would I, but I'm not sure everyone will believe that. They don't know me, after all."

"Hmph. I just met you and I can already tell you're not a

cheater."

"Thank you. But not everyone will give me the benefit of the doubt."

"Maybe the three of you should go out together. That would probably silence most of the wagging tongues."

"You know, that's a good idea. I'll talk to Logan about it."

Their food arrived and the four of them talked throughout the meal. Before leaving, Honey and Cici made plans to see each other again. Honey promised to show Cici her barrel-racing operation.

"That was fun," Cici said on the way home. "It's nice to meet other couples. Do you know all the Gallaghers well?"

"Since we were kids. Jack, Sean, and Wyatt are doctors at our hospital. Glenna is married to a PI. She and Dylan run the ranch. Dylan breeds Norwegian Fjords. He's married to one of the trauma surgeons, Samantha Striker."

"Sounds like almost everyone in that family is involved in medicine."

"Most of them are."

"Do you like being a surgeon? You've never talked about it much. Other than that one time you told me about your patient."

"Obviously, I don't like it when people die. But yeah, most of the time I like it. What about you? Do you like being a writer?"

"It depends."

"On what?"

"Whether my writing is going well, whether my deadline is too close, and I don't think I'll make it." She sighed. "Writer's block is a bitch. When writing is good it's really good. And when it's bad it's…the shits."

He laughed. "Very descriptive."

"I *am* a writer, you know."

"Yes, you are."

"Do you want to stay tonight?" she asked when they pulled up to her place.

"Yes, but I'd better not. I have an early day tomorrow. But I can come in for a little while."

"Good," she said, leaning over and kissing him.

THE IDEA HADN'T come to Logan suddenly. He'd been thinking about it for a while now. Honestly, almost since the day he and Cici had finally gotten together. But he knew he was rushing it.

He and Cici had only been together in public for a little more than two weeks. Secretly for longer but they still hadn't known each other all that long. Logan wanted Cici. Not just for now, not for a while, but for good. He wanted to marry her. And Logan was very good at going after what he wanted.

Hell, he hadn't even told her he loved her. She knew she was more to him than a fling. They'd talked about 'falling for' each other. But he didn't think she knew how serious he was about the two of them. When he thought of the future, he saw Cici in his. But did she feel the same?

His only serious relationship had cratered when he discovered the woman he loved wasn't who he thought she was. He'd backed her up, been totally on her side, until he'd finally had to admit the truth. She was a cheat and a liar. Oh, she hadn't cheated on him sexually but she'd tried to cheat the internship and residency program. Which was bad enough, but when he learned she'd tried to frame another resident for her mistakes, he'd been appalled. How had he trusted her? He hadn't been tempted to do anything long term since. But he was thirty-four. It was time to get over the past and plan a future with Cici.

She might not be ready. Just because he was crazy in love with her didn't mean she felt the same urgency he did. And if she didn't, she'd tell him. He knew she cared about him. He could wait. If he had to.

He went to Bozeman to find a ring. If he tried to find one in Marietta, or even Livingston, everyone in town would know his plans before he even popped the question. A very nice older lady helped him choose the ring. He ended up with a round-cut diamond surrounded by smaller diamonds in a platinum setting. If Cici didn't like it or it didn't fit they could bring it back to size or exchange it. Now all he had to do was find the right place and time to ask her. It needed to be soon because waiting was only making him more nervous.

He made reservations that night at the fancy new Galveston Steak House that was the Texas entrepreneur Atticus Bowen's brainchild. The historic building had been the Bank of Marietta until it was remodeled into a steakhouse recently. It was a striking, unusual restaurant with lots of white marble, fancy columns, a black-and-white marble floor, and high ceilings. The food was excellent, the wine list unique, and the ambience romantic, making it the perfect place, Logan decided, to ask Cici to marry him.

CICI HAD DRESSED carefully. In fact, she'd torn through her clothes trying to find the perfect outfit. Tonight was going to be special. She could feel it. Logan was taking her to the new steakhouse on Main Street. Formerly a historic bank, the restaurant was said to be absolutely gorgeous. Cici was looking forward to seeing it.

She wound up wearing a new dress, a classic little black dress that wrapped around her closely, with a plunging neckline, short cap sleeves, and a hem stopping several inches above her knees. She added sheer black thigh-high hose and barely there high-heeled black sandals, a diamond drop around her neck, and dangly earrings. Her makeup accented her eyes, making them appear wider and more sultry, and the finishing touch was fire-engine red lipstick. Non-smear, of course.

She'd run around like a crazy person, picking up the plethora of clothes she'd strewn everywhere in her attempt to find the perfect dress. Realizing it would take too long to hang everything, she simply stuffed it all into her closet. At least she could let Logan in without making him wonder if a bomb had gone off.

"Hi," she said when she opened the door to Logan's knock.

He said nothing. He stared at her looking…dumbstruck was the only word she could think of. "You look gorgeous," he finally said.

"Thanks. I was beginning to wonder if I'd forgotten something. You look nice too." He wore a navy coat with a pale gray shirt, gray pants, and no tie. She'd never seen him in anything but scrubs or blue jeans and casual shirts but he really rocked dress clothes too.

She grabbed her black lacy shawl, and let Logan place it over her shoulders. It was pretty but not terribly warm. "Are you going to tell me what this special occasion is about?"

"Eventually." He looked at her and sighed. "I really want to kiss you but I suspect we'd never make it to the restaurant if I did."

She laughed. "You're not getting out of it that easily. I'm dying to see this place."

It was everything she'd heard about and more. There was a plaque outside saying it was a historical landmark that was formerly the Bank of Marietta. When she walked in she was stunned at how beautiful it was. White marble was everywhere. Fancy columns, a patterned black-and-white marble floor, and a gorgeous, intricate ceiling.

There was modern art hanging on the walls, splashes of color livening all the white marble. There were booths covered in sapphire velvet and tables scattered throughout.

The hostess led them to one of the tables that was tucked away, almost as if it was in a private room. She gave them the menus and left after asking if they wanted a drink besides water. Cici ordered a glass of white wine and Logan ordered red.

Strains of classical music could be heard in the background. The lighting was low, lending a sumptuous air to the restaurant. "This is awfully romantic," Cici said.

"That's why I brought you here."

"You seem…different tonight," she told him. "If I didn't know better I'd say you were nervous." She'd never known Logan to be nervous. It didn't seem to go with his personality. He was a surgeon, after all. They weren't known to be nervous types.

He smiled but didn't comment. Their server came with their drinks and Logan asked for more time before they ordered dinner.

"You've gone to a lot of trouble," Cici said. "Is there a reason for that?"

He took her hand and held it. "Yes."

He didn't say any more. "Logan, what is going on?"

"What do you want for dinner? Steak, seafood, something else?"

Fine. He wasn't talking. She pulled her hand away and picked up the menu. Everything looked good. She'd made up her mind quickly but she pretended she hadn't. Whatever he was doing it was irritating the snot out of her.

The waiter came back and they gave him their orders. "I'll have the house salad, a small filet medium rare, and the seasonal vegetables," Cici said.

"I'd like the rib eye medium rare, house potatoes, and a Caesar salad." To Cici he said, "Are you sure you don't want an appetizer?"

"No, this is plenty."

Not long after that their salads came and then the entrees. Logan never did tell her what was going on but he was being so sweet and romantic she got over her snit. Maybe he'd just wanted to do something nice for her. But if so, why had he acted like there was more to it?

Eventually they returned to her apartment. She took off her coat and hung it up.

"Come sit on the couch with me," he said. "There's something I need to tell you." When they sat he picked up her hand and held it. "I know I said I'd fallen for you but that wasn't exactly true."

Uh-oh. That didn't sound good. She didn't speak.

"I love you, Cici."

"Oh, thank God. I thought you were going to break up with me."

"Why would I take you to a romantic restaurant if that was what I was going to do?"

"I didn't say it was reasonable."

Looking perplexed, he shook his head. She put her arms around his neck and kissed him. "I'm glad because I love you too."

"Good, because there's something I want to ask you. I was going to ask you at dinner but I decided it would be better at home."

"What?"

He let her go and pulled something out of his pocket. It was a small velvet box. A jewelry box. Her eyes widened and she couldn't have spoken on a bet. He opened it and there was a beautiful diamond ring inside. Her heart pounded so hard she almost couldn't hear him.

"I love you, Cici. Will you marry me?"

She simply stared at him, totally, completely blown away.

When she didn't answer he said, "We haven't known each other that long but I've known I wanted to spend my life with you since I found out the truth about you and Liam. Honestly, even before that, but I knew that was a pipe dream with you involved with my brother."

"I—I don't know what to say." Her head was spinning.

"Is yes out of the question?"

"Oh, Logan. Are you sure?"

"Yes, but you obviously aren't."

"It's not that. I told you I love you too and I meant it. But I can't marry you. Not yet."

"It's too soon, isn't it?"

No, it wasn't too soon. The minute he asked her she knew there was nothing else she'd rather do than marry Logan McFarland. But she couldn't. Not until she told him about her past. Her parents. That was far too big a secret to keep from the man you were going to marry. He didn't even know her real name.

"We've only known each other a few months. We—we don't need to rush into anything."

He closed the ring box and tucked it away. "Is this no for good or no for now?"

"For now."

"We could be engaged. For as long as you want."

"I'm just…not ready. I'm sorry." Not until she told him her secret. And once she did would he understand why she'd kept her past a secret? She didn't know but she knew that until she told Logan about her past they couldn't move forward. And she didn't want to do that tonight.

"Don't be. I knew it was too soon."

That wasn't the real problem. But she wasn't ready to tell him the real reason for the delay. "Will you stay?"

"I'm not sure I should."

"Please?" She stood and took his hand, tugging him up to stand beside her, then led him to her bed. "I want to make love with you."

Chapter Nineteen

HE SHOULD RESIST her. Leave her alone to think things over. He shouldn't have been surprised. He was an idiot to ask her so soon. But she was it for him. She was the woman he wanted to spend the rest of his life with. He shrugged out of his coat and laid it over a chair.

She turned her back to him so that he could unzip her. He did and she turned around and let her dress drop to pool at her feet. She kicked it aside. She stood there in a black, lacy demi-cup bra, tiny black lace panties, thigh-high black hose and her high-heeled black sandals. He'd never seen her look sexier. Hell, he'd never seen anyone else as sexy as Cici was.

Cici sat on the bed and began to take off her shoes but Logan stopped her. "Leave them. And the hose." He was surprised he could speak; his voice came out husky and rough.

She smiled and reached for his belt buckle. Very slowly she divested him of his belt, his pants, his boxers. When he was naked she picked up a condom packet, opened it and fit it over his iron-hard cock. She stood and her gaze locked with his. She took off her bra and let her breasts spill out. Then she lay back on the bed, crooked one leg, and said, "What are you waiting for?"

There was no more talk after that. And there was no way he could go slowly. He landed beside her on the bed, ripped off her panties, then rolled over until he was poised above her. He kissed her, desperate to get inside her. With one fast thrust, he drove inside her, groaning and pausing as he felt her slick inner walls tighten around him. He began to move, pounding inside her, pulling almost all the way out and plunging inside her again. And again.

His orgasm built, then blew sky high at the same time he heard her cry and her body tightened, gloving him, demanding everything he had to give. Eventually, he rolled aside, taking her with him to cuddle against him side by side.

It took him a while before he could think again. Why had he fallen in love with Cici so quickly? She was beautiful but he'd known other beautiful women. She was smart, but he'd always been attracted to smart women. She was honest. As soon as she knew she and Liam weren't going to work, she'd told his brother. Up front. She'd agreed to Liam's ruse because she felt she owed it to him and because she knew how important it was to Liam. And even though she said she'd had feelings for Logan almost since they met, she hadn't let on until she cleared it with Liam. She knew Logan wouldn't betray his brother.

He did wonder occasionally about why Cici had left

Texas and had been so determined to leave it all behind her. But he knew she'd tell him. They just hadn't gotten around to it yet. Of course, he hadn't told her everything about his past either. Nothing about Janelle and for sure nothing about Beth, the major reason it had taken him so long to find a woman he wanted to risk loving again.

"What are you thinking about?" Cici asked him. She lay on his chest, both of them naked since he'd eventually taken off her hose and shoes after making love to her.

"You. That I love you," he answered truthfully.

Forearms on his chest, she rose up and kissed him. "You'd never said that until tonight."

"You knew I was crazy about you."

"I hoped you were."

"I figured your first clue would have been the fact I've been spending every spare moment with you."

"You could have just liked the sex."

"I did. I do. But there's a lot more between us than just sex." At least, he hoped like hell there was. There was no question on his part.

"I'm glad. I love you too, Logan."

He bit back the obvious question. *If you love me why didn't you say you'd marry me? Why wait?*

LOGAN COULDN'T BLAME Cici for not immediately saying

yes to his proposal but it still bothered him. He wasn't saying they had to get married immediately but he didn't see why they couldn't get engaged. She hadn't even considered that. Just 'I'm not ready.' They loved each other. Neither one of them was terribly young. He was in his thirties and she was in her late twenties, maybe even early thirties. He realized he didn't know her exact age. It was on her profile but he hadn't ever looked at that. No, they hadn't known each other for a long time, but he thought they knew each other pretty well.

He'd had a call early that morning about a possible appendectomy but he still had a bit of time before he had to head to the hospital when his phone rang. Checking caller ID, he saw it was Byron Phillips, an old friend he'd gone to medical school with until Byron dropped out their third year. He and Byron had kept in touch sporadically through the years but it had been a while since he'd heard from him.

"Hey, Byron, how's it going? Haven't talked to you in a while."

"Phone works both ways." They both laughed.

They shot the shit for a little while then Byron said, "I'll get right to it. Liz and I are pregnant."

"Congratulations, man. Do you know whether it's a boy or a girl? When is it due?" He knew they'd been trying for some time so it was welcome news.

"A boy. She's seven and a half months along. Which is why I'm calling you now. Liz and I want you to be his godfather. What do you say? Think you can make it down here?" Byron and his wife lived in Fort Worth now.

"Absolutely. I'm honored but are you sure there's no one there you'd rather have?"

"No one. I haven't forgotten what you did for me all those years ago when the shit hit the fan."

"It was nothing." Byron and his family had been scammed and lost most of their money when Byron was in his third year of medical school. It had resulted in him dropping out and looking for a job. Logan had let him stay in his apartment with him rent-free until his friend could find a job and get back on his feet. If he'd had enough money himself he'd have lent it to his friend to finish med school, but as it was Logan had been working his way through school and had a boatload of student debt. Byron wound up being a very successful entrepreneur whose company specialized in developing and distributing cutting-edge medical equipment.

"Bullshit. You saved my life, buddy."

"An exaggeration, but I'm glad everything turned out okay."

"It did. I really like what I'm doing."

"Business is booming, huh?"

Byron laughed. "It is at that. Anything new with you? You seeing anyone?"

Byron's wife had tried to set him up with friends of hers several times. They both thought he should find a good woman and settle down. Logan had gone out with a couple of them but after that he resisted.

"As a matter of fact, yes. I've been seeing a woman here. We're getting serious." At least, he hoped they were. "She's from Fort Worth originally. Just moved up here not too long ago."

"Anyone I'd know?"

"Possibly. You might know of her, anyway. Cici Bradley. She's a writer."

There was a long silence. "You still there?" Logan asked.

"Does she write thrillers?"

"Yeah. Have you read her books?"

Byron didn't answer that directly. "Cici Bradley is her pen name, right?"

"Yeah. But that's what she goes by. Why?"

"I'm assuming you don't know her real name, then."

His voice sounded odd. Strained, as if he was having difficulty speaking. "No, it hasn't come up. At first I wondered but I figured she'd tell me at some point." Honestly, it hadn't mattered to him.

"Her real name is Cecelia Owen."

Why was that familiar? "Owen? Isn't that—" No, it was just a coincidence. It had to be.

"Yeah, it is. She's part of the family who scammed us. She and her parents with their Ponzi scheme."

Logan closed his eyes, a sick feeling in his stomach. "You're shitting me."

"Nope. Hand to God."

"You're saying Cici was involved in the scam? I knew they had a daughter but I thought she wasn't involved."

"Maybe not. But it was never proven she had nothing to do with it."

"There wasn't proof she had anything to do with it either, was there?"

"Not proof, no. She didn't go to prison like her parents did, but if she wasn't actually a part of it she had to have known about it. It's common thinking that she sold out her parents rather than go to prison herself."

"I—I can't believe this." Cici, involved in a Ponzi scheme? He couldn't imagine her doing that. Or being involved in anything criminal. Not the woman he knew. "Are you sure?"

"Damn sure. Cici Bradley is Cecelia Owen's pen name. It's her, Logan."

"I don't know what to say."

"Ask her if you don't believe me. Or hell, look it up on the internet."

"I'm not saying I don't believe you. But I can't reconcile the woman I know with her being a criminal."

"She's playing you, man. Be careful."

They hung up not long after that. Logan didn't know what to think. He didn't know what to do. He looked at the time and realized he had to get to the hospital. This would have to wait. He was suddenly glad he had work and wouldn't have to think about it for a while.

LOGAN FINALLY FINISHED at the hospital late that night. Not only had the appendectomy been more complex given the appendix had burst, but he had two other cases that were difficult as well. By the time he finished he was exhausted but he knew it would be hard to sleep until he found out the truth of what Byron had told him. It would have to wait until morning, though, since it was midnight already and Liam would be long asleep.

He needed to talk to Cici, but first he wanted to see what Liam knew. Or didn't know. He called Liam early the next morning since he knew his brother got up before dawn.

"What's up?" Liam asked.

"It's me."

"I know. It's awfully early for you unless you're working. What's wrong?"

"I'll tell you when I get there."

"You sound weird. Is it work? Or is something wrong with you and Cici?"

"Not work. I'll know more once I talk to you. I'll meet you at the barn. I don't want Mom to hear this."

Twenty minutes later he pulled up to the ranch house and walked down to the barn. Rambler greeted him enthusiastically. "Down, Rambler." Damn, he needed to work with him. He was picking up bad habits from the other dogs. They were all barn dogs and while they were good dogs their manners weren't the best. Logan petted him and rubbed under his chin the way he liked. He missed his dog but he also knew Rambler loved the ranch and the freedom he had there. Besides, he couldn't keep him at his apartment. Even when he found a house with a yard he'd have to find someone to look in on him when he was working. Or bring him out to stay at the ranch.

But for now he needed to find out what Liam knew about Cici and her parents. Liam was in Riptide's stall, talking to the horse. His brother had a magic touch with horses. He loved them and they knew it. Logan liked horses and didn't mind pitching in on the ranch work when he could, but that wasn't often, especially now that he lived in town. He understood a little better now why Connor had a hard time showing up to help.

"Hey," he said to Liam.

"Hey. What's up?"

"I need to talk to you."

"Okay. What are you doing calling me at the crack of dawn?"

"I'm about to tell you." Or rather, ask him.

"Want a drink? There are some Cokes in the tack room." They walked in and Liam opened the small refrigerator and pulled out two Cokes, tossing Logan one of them. Liam didn't say any more, just waited for him to talk.

Logan took a long drink of his Coke. "Do you know Cici's real name? Not her author name but the real one?"

"No, why?"

"Do you remember my friend Byron? I knew him in medical school."

"Yeah. Didn't he live with you for a while?"

"He did. After his family lost all their money in a Ponzi scheme."

Liam swallowed some of his drink and leaned back against the desk. "What does Byron have to do with Cici? And why do you want to know her real name?"

"Byron told me her real name is Cecelia Owen."

"Okay. So?"

"Cecelia Owen is the daughter of the people who ran that Ponzi scheme. The one that screwed over Byron and his family."

Liam was silent for a moment. "He's sure of that?"

"Yeah. And on top of that Byron thinks Cici was involved in the scam."

Liam stared at him. "Cici? Bullshit. Cici wouldn't be involved in something like that." He paused. "You're not telling me you believe it?"

"I don't know what to believe." He finished his drink and tossed it at the trash can. Naturally, he missed. "Byron is convinced she took part in it. He thinks she made a deal to give up her parents so she wouldn't go to prison."

"Byron's wrong," Liam said decisively. "I don't know anything about her parents but I know Cici. She wouldn't be a part of a Ponzi scheme. Ripping people off? No."

Logan shook his head. He didn't want to believe Byron but at the least her parents had started it. Byron had said they'd both gone to prison. "Her father must have died in prison. Did she tell you that?"

"No. I thought you were in love with her?"

"I am."

"How can you be in love with her and not trust her? Don't you know her at all? Hell, I'm not in love with her and I know she wouldn't be part of a Ponzi scheme."

Whenever he thought about trusting a woman completely, especially when there were questions, he thought of Beth. He'd thought she was trustworthy. He'd been madly in love with her. So much so that when she'd been accused of falsifying patient data he'd been solidly behind her. Only to find out she was guilty. The only other woman he'd been serious about was his girlfriend when he was a in high school. He'd thought they were exclusive. Janelle hadn't. She'd slept with one of his friends.

"I don't *want* to believe it. But you didn't see the destruction it caused. You didn't live with Byron who had to drop out of med school and look for a job that would support him. Or hear about his parents and what happened to them."

"That's on her parents, not her."

"I hope you're right." But what if it was true? What if Cici unwittingly was a part of the scam? He wouldn't— couldn't believe she'd been part of it deliberately. But maybe she'd been duped too.

But if she had been duped, or had no part in it, why not tell him about it? She'd never even told Liam and him her real name. Probably because she was afraid someone would recognize it and she'd be forced to tell them about the scam.

"She never mentioned anything about this to you?" he asked Liam.

Liam shook his head. "What are you going to do?"

"Talk to her." And hope she had a good explanation for what had happened and why she hadn't told him.

Chapter Twenty

CICI WAS WORKING on her book when someone pounded on her door. Her deadline was drawing near and it was crunch time. She sighed, knowing it was almost certainly one of two people. Logan or Letty. Logan had texted her earlier saying he was going to the ranch so it was probably Letty.

"Cici, let me in."

Logan. She opened the door. "Hi. I thought you were at the ranch helping Liam."

He stalked in. Stalked. That was the only word for it. "I was."

"What's wrong?" she asked when that was all he said. "Is it work? Is it about the ranch, or your family?"

He'd begun pacing and now he stopped, shoving a hand through his hair. Alarmed now, she waited.

"I don't want to believe it. But Byron is so sure."

"Who's Byron?"

He ignored her question. Instead he asked one of his own. "What's your real name?"

"You mean—"

"Your real name. Not your pen name."

Her heart rate sped up. The way he asked that said it wasn't an idle question. "Cecelia Owen. Why?"

"Any relation to the Owens who ran the Ponzi scheme in Fort Worth?"

Shit! Oh, shit. Why hadn't she told him? Someone else had obviously dropped that bomb. As soon as he'd asked her to marry him she'd known she had to tell him. But she'd put it off for a little while, trying to figure out the best way to approach the subject. Just bring it up out of the blue? Lead up to it somehow? But that didn't matter. Now it was too late. She sat down heavily on the couch. "Yes. My parents. Who told you?"

Once again he ignored her. "Were you a part of it?"

Shocked, she stared at him. "No! How could you think I'd be involved in something like that?" Surely he knew her better than that.

He sat, as far away from her as he could manage on her small couch.

Maybe he didn't.

"I don't want to think it. But I got a phone call from an old friend of mine. Both he and his parents were scammed several years ago. By your parents."

She closed her eyes, then opened them to look at Logan. "Oh, God. I'm so sorry, Logan." More people whose lives her parents had ruined.

"When I told Byron about you he recognized your pen

name. He told me who you really were. I felt like an idiot when I admitted I didn't know your real name. I wondered at times, but it never seemed that important."

"I would have told you if you'd asked. But you never did."

"Byron thinks you were involved."

"I wasn't. I knew nothing about it. But there are a lot of people in Fort Worth who don't believe that. Obviously your friend is one of them." She paused and stared at him. "You believe I was involved." She didn't blame his friend. After all, her parents had ruined his life. He had no reason to believe she was innocent. Even the fact that she hadn't gone to prison didn't necessarily mean she was innocent of any involvement. But Logan was her lover. He'd asked her to marry him, for God's sake. He should know her better.

He stood and began to pace. "I don't know what to believe. Byron thinks you made some kind of deal. Turning in your parents so you wouldn't be charged."

Why was he so quick to believe the worst of her? Because he obviously did. "If that's what you think, you don't know me at all." If it hadn't been for her friend Fran coming to her with her suspicions Cici would never have known about any of it. Sure, she'd wondered how her parents could afford the houses, the cars, the expensive vacations, the jewelry. But she'd believed their investment business was legit.

"How did you prove you weren't involved?"

"You don't believe me." Her heart hurt. That Logan

could believe the worst of her… "How can you even be with me if that's what you think of me?"

"That's not an answer."

Anger superseded the hurt. She'd told him she had nothing to do with it. If that wasn't good enough for him, he could go to hell.

"It's all the answer you're going to get." She felt tears starting but she willed them back. She wouldn't let him know how much he'd hurt her.

"I haven't said I believed you had a hand in it. I wanted an explanation. I can't just blindly believe anything you tell me."

"Do you honestly believe I'm a scam artist?"

"No, but you could have been involved unwittingly."

So he thought she was stupid along with being a criminal. Her heart felt like it was torn in two. But it manifested in anger. "You need to leave."

"I don't want to leave. I want to believe you. I don't—I don't think you were involved."

"You just admitted you do. At the least you think it's possible." She walked to the door and opened it. Stood there while he stared at her.

"Cici—"

She shook her head. "Just go, Logan."

He walked out the door, turned and started to speak. Cici closed the door in his face. She couldn't stand there a moment longer without dissolving completely.

A COUPLE OF days later Cici still felt like a boulder was sitting on her chest. Each morning when she woke she wondered why and then it all came crashing back. Logan thought she was a criminal. A stupid criminal, yet. Damn him! She'd told him the truth and he hadn't believed her. Even if she convinced him of her innocence how could they be together when she knew what he really thought of her? What he'd been so damned quick to believe.

She was sitting in front of her computer staring at a blank page when someone knocked. She didn't answer it. She thought Logan had worked the night before so he'd be off. He was the last person she wanted to see.

"Cici, open up. It's Liam."

She wasn't sure she wanted to see Liam either but she opened the door.

He looked her over, then walked in. "My brother is a complete dumbass. He came down on you, didn't he?"

"You could say that. I'm assuming Logan told you all about my parents and what they did. The Ponzi scheme—and that he believes I had a part in it." She sat on the couch and waved a hand at him.

"He did." He took a seat next to her.

"I'm sure you hate me as much as Logan does."

"What? I don't hate you. And I'm sure Logan doesn't either."

"Yes, he does. He walked in a couple of days ago thinking I was a criminal and then he walked out thinking I was either a criminal or totally stupid or both." She sniffed, holding on to her mad.

"Cici, anyone who knows you knows you wouldn't be a party to a scam. Logan knows it too. He's just being a dumb shit."

"He thinks I turned my parents in so I wouldn't get charged."

"Did you?"

"What do you think?"

"I think if you turned them in it was because what they were doing was wrong."

"Thanks. I told Logan that but he wasn't interested. He said he wanted an explanation but really, he'd already made up his mind."

"He's been burned before. I think that's why he's being so clueless."

"What happened?" She knew basically nothing about Logan's past. Maybe he had a good reason for believing the worst about her. Except he should know her better than that.

"That's his story to tell. But it would go a long way to explaining his current behavior."

"He called last night but I didn't pick up."

"You don't have to talk to him unless you want to."

"I don't want to." She got up. "Do you want some water? I don't have anything else."

"Water would be good. Thanks."

She returned and handed him a bottle. She took a drink of her own water. "Why are you here, Liam?"

"After Logan told me what happened night before last I had a feeling he was going to screw things up. I figured you needed a friend."

"I do. Why are you so nice to me?"

He shrugged. "I like you. And I'm responsible for you being here. I'm not responsible for Logan being a dumbass though."

She sighed. "No, you're not. It's not so much that he's upset about what happened. I understand that. I should have told him but I put it off. But he jumped to the worst conclusion possible and he didn't believe me when I told him I hadn't known anything about it. I guess I could have gone into more of an explanation but the way he was acting it didn't seem worth it."

"It would have been so much easier if you'd fallen for me instead of Logan."

"Yes, but I didn't. Besides, you didn't fall for me either."

"No, but I think I could have."

She didn't know what to say to that. "Liam, I—"

He held up a hand. "Don't worry. I'm not hitting on you. For one thing, Logan is still stuck on you."

"Is he? I'm not so sure of that." And even if he was, she couldn't simply forgive him as if nothing had happened. "Besides, if that's what he really thinks of me I don't want to be with him."

Chapter Twenty-One

WORK WAS SAVING him. Without it he'd have gone crazy trying to figure out what he should do. As it was he thought about Cici whenever he wasn't working. The problem, or part of it, was that he was still angry. And hurt. Cici clearly didn't trust him. Otherwise she'd have told him her real name, at the least.

Had she ever planned to tell him about her family? Now that he thought about it, now that he knew the truth, everything she'd done made sense. Leaving Fort Worth. Hell, leaving the state. Coming to Montana to start over. Going by her pen name. Not telling Liam anything either.

He didn't honestly believe Cici had been involved in the scam, no matter what Byron thought. But had she known about it? Had she turned in her parents because they were criminals? Or had she only turned them in because she'd been wrongly accused and she wanted to save herself?

Shit. That didn't sound like the woman he knew either. But he'd been wrong before. Terribly wrong in believing in a woman. In two women. He and Janelle had both been young so he could be forgiven for not seeing who she really was.

But Beth... He'd been an adult. In his residency. An adult who'd been blind to her true nature. You'd think he'd have learned.

He'd tried to call Cici but she wasn't answering his calls. Which also pissed him off. He was the injured party here. The one who'd been kept in the dark. She should have told him when he asked her to marry him. Or even before that, when they started getting serious. Unless she hadn't meant to tell him at all.

Or maybe she hadn't been as serious about him as he'd been about her. After all, she hadn't said she'd marry him.

He hadn't seen Cici or talked to her in over a week. He hadn't seen Liam either, except when he'd first found out. But he'd talked to him once after that. Liam—his brother, for God's sake—was clearly on Cici's side. He'd asked Logan when he was going to get over being a dumbass and make up with Cici. Good thing they'd been on the phone or Logan would have punched him.

News of his and Cici's breakup was all over the hospital just as news about the two of them getting together had been earlier. He ran into one of the nurses he'd gone out with a few weeks before Liam had brought Cici to town. Literally ran into her.

"Sorry, Lanie. I wasn't looking where I was going."

"No worries, Logan." She smiled and put her hand on his arm. "I heard you and Cici broke up."

"Yes." He said it in his most repressive tone but that

didn't seem to bother Lanie.

"Why don't we go to dinner one night? I sure had a good time the last time we went out."

He didn't really remember but he supposed it hadn't been bad or he would have. "Thanks, but I'm taking a break from dating for a while."

"Oh," she said, pouting. "Well, if you change your mind you know my number."

Lanie was a nice woman but it was impossible to think about another woman when he was still hung up on the one who'd broken up with him.

HER DEADLINE WAS the only thing keeping her even a little bit sane. Cici could escape into her book where the stakes were fictional life and death and not think about the fact that Logan had broken her heart. But she couldn't work constantly.

And when she wasn't working she'd cried until she was sick to death of it. She hadn't gone to her volunteer job because she hadn't wanted to run into Logan. She hadn't gone anywhere else except the grocery store for the same reason. For the last two weeks she'd subsisted on pizza delivered to the apartment, microwave meals, and junk food. Enough was enough, she decided. Logan McFarland was going to regret what he'd done and if he dared to want her back she would crush him like a bug.

In that militant mood she called Letty and asked her to meet her at the Main Street Diner for lunch.

"Sure," Letty said. "I've been wondering where you were since I haven't seen you for days but then I remembered your deadline and figured you were working."

Cici mumbled an agreement, decided to wait until she saw her friend before telling her what had happened. When she arrived at the diner, she sat in her car and waited, calling herself a coward, but luckily Letty was right on time so they could walk in together.

She led the way to a booth in the back. The Main Street Diner was old-fashioned, with red brick walls and a wooden floor, the stools at the counter as well as the booths covered in red vinyl. They both ordered hamburgers and fries. That seemed to be their go-to. Letty had a ridiculously high metabolism and stayed very slender and Cici didn't give a shit at the moment about her diet. Hell, she'd been living on junk food and pizza for days. Losing those five pounds would keep.

"All right, what's going on?" Letty asked after they got their drinks.

"That obvious, huh?"

"I don't want to hurt your feelings but you look like shit."

Cici choked on her tea. "Thanks," she said when she recovered.

"You're welcome. Now what happened?"

"Logan and I broke up."

"Damn. I was hoping it wasn't something like that. Why? I thought you were crazy about each other."

"We were. Until he heard about my past."

Their food arrived and Letty waited until they'd both eaten some before asking, "What happened in your past?"

She proceeded to tell Letty the whole miserable story. Unlike Logan, Letty didn't immediately assume Cici had known about her parents' scam. But then, she listened rather than coming at her with both barrels blazing. Asking instead of accusing her like Logan had.

When she finished, Letty was quiet for a moment, then asked, "Does Logan really believe you'd be involved in something like that?"

"I don't know. He says he doesn't know what to believe." She looked at her friend. "What about you? What do you think?"

"I think Logan is a dumbass." She ate a french fry and sat back.

Cici agreed. "That's what Liam said too."

"Liam believes you?"

"He does. Which makes Logan's reaction even worse." Though she really wasn't hungry, she ate a bit more. "So you don't think I took part in it?"

Letty stared at her with her mouth open, then laughed. "You? Of course not."

"Too bad Logan doesn't have your faith in me."

"Have you talked to him since your blowup?"

"No. He's called several times but I haven't answered." The latest being two days before. She'd been so tempted to answer.

"Maybe you should talk to him. He might have a reason for being um, unsure."

"Oh, right. What kind of reason could he have? Other than he has absolutely no faith in me."

"Maybe he's been burned before. Do you know anything about his past relationships?"

Cici shook her head. "Nothing. It's never come up."

"Well, to be fair you haven't known each other that long."

"Long enough for him to ask me to marry him."

Letty sat up straight. "Holy crap! You're kidding."

"No, it was before he heard about my parents. I put him off. Which was a damn good thing. But I knew I couldn't agree to marry him until I told him the truth about my past. Only I didn't get a chance. His friend told him before I could."

"That sucks."

It certainly did.

"Do you love him?"

Cici ordered herself not to cry. It didn't work. She nodded miserably as tears rolled down her cheeks.

Letty patted her hand. "That answers that question. Do

you want my advice?"

"Yes."

"Talk to him. This happened what, a couple of weeks ago? You've both had time to think. See what he has to say."

"I don't know what to do if he apologizes for jumping to the wrong conclusion. It's not that I can't forgive him. I can, but I don't see how we move on from here."

"Just talk to him. See what happens."

"I'll think about it." *He doesn't trust me. He doesn't even know what type of person I am. How am I supposed to be with a man who thinks I could be a criminal? Not only that, but a criminal who benefits from taking people's hard-earned money?*

"Speak of the devil, look who just walked in."

Cici looked up and met Logan's gaze. Dammit, this was the last thing she needed.

"He's coming over," Letty said.

She panicked, about to get up and flee, but Letty put her hand on her arm. "You might as well talk to him. You'll have to at some point."

She sucked in a breath and watched him as he came toward her. Why did he have to look so good when she looked like a piece of crap? It wasn't fair.

"Cici, Letty," he said, nodding at them. "How are you?"

Cici said nothing. She couldn't speak. Letty answered. "Fine. How are you, Logan?"

"Not so good. Cici, can we talk?"

"I'd rather not." There, she'd finally managed to say

something. It gave her strength to continue. "I don't see that we have anything to talk about."

"We have a lot to talk about. First of all, I'm sorry. Will you let me explain?"

He looked so sincere. So regretful. As if he thought he could apologize and everything would go back to the way it was. But it wouldn't. "I can't do this here. Just…leave me alone, Logan."

His brows drew together. He was angry but that was too damn bad.

"I will. For now." He turned on his heel and left.

"Was that as awful as I think it was?" she asked Letty.

"Yes."

Trust Letty to tell her the truth.

THAT WENT WELL. She wouldn't even allow him a chance to explain. When she'd looked and their gazes met all of his feelings, every damned mixed one he'd had since this mess happened crashed into him. And over it all the one unavoidable fact. He still loved her.

He'd screwed up completely. He shouldn't have come at Cici with accusations. *Asking* her what had happened would have been better. But the whole situation was far too similar to his experience with Beth years ago. He'd believed everything Beth told him. Thought she was completely innocent.

And he couldn't have been more wrong.

And he'd learned from that experience. Hell, he hadn't been involved seriously since. Until he met Cici and fell crazy in love with her. So crazy that he couldn't tell the truth from a lie? Cici was nothing like Beth. He knew that, so how could he have suspected she'd been part of a fraudulent scheme?

And what about Liam? Liam believed her and he was no fool. He also wasn't a suspicious son of a bitch like Logan was, even after being jilted at the altar. After all, Liam was the one who'd brought Cici to Marietta through a dating app. He was the one who'd gotten to know Cici first.

Logan had let his friendship and experience with Byron as well as his experience with Beth color what he knew to be true about Cici. But he kept coming back to how Beth had fooled him. Was he so enamored of Cici that she could be a completely different person than he thought she was?

Logan was due at the hospital in half an hour. He couldn't afford to be stewing about Cici when he had patients. Patients who needed him. Operations that needed his full attention. *Lock it away. Think about it when you have time but for now, lock it away.*

That only worked for so long. As long as he was in the hospital and busy, he was okay. But when he got home he couldn't stop thinking. About Cici. About the whole mess. It had been more than two weeks since their blowup. He didn't know if that was enough time for her but it was for him.

He'd been wrong to accuse her before he even heard her side of the matter.

He called her. It went to voice mail. He left a message. *Cici, I'm sorry. Can we talk?*

She didn't respond. Neither that time nor any of the times during the next few days that he called. Was she ever going to allow him to explain? Or was he doomed to keep trying until even he got the picture?

Chapter Twenty-Two

LOGAN FINALLY FIGURED out if he wanted to talk to Cici he was going to have to go to her apartment and hope she'd let him in. He'd run into her a couple of times in person, the latest being at the Main Street Diner when she told him to leave her alone. As for the phone, forget about it. Honestly, it pissed him off. It wasn't as if she'd explained anything beyond saying she hadn't been involved.

But then, he hadn't explained anything either. Too caught up with the here and now, the sizzling attraction between them, they'd never really talked about their pasts. It was time they did. Assuming Cici let him in the door.

Her car was at her apartment, a good sign that she'd be home. He knocked on the door.

"Who is it?"

"It's Logan. Can we talk?"

It took her a while but she finally cracked open the door. "What is there to talk about?"

"Let me in and I'll tell you."

Grudgingly, she let him in. Her hair was piled up on her head with some kind of clip, more to get it out of her way than as a fashion statement. She wore sweatpants and an old, faded gray T-shirt with a graphic of an alligator below printing that read *Jazzfest*. Her computer was open on the table, several books were open and strewn about, telling him she'd clearly been writing.

"Sorry. Am I interrupting?"

She shrugged. "What do you want?"

"To tell you I'm sorry about what happened. About how I responded when I heard about your family. I should have listened to you rather than accusing you."

"Yes, you should have. Is that all?"

"No, that's not all. Give me a break here, Cici. Can we talk about this like adults?"

She shrugged again. "All right. Sit down." She waved at the couch.

"I think I need to explain where I'm coming from." She simply looked at him. "I'm not denying I was wrong to react like I did but there were…extenuating circumstances." Cici raised an eyebrow as if to say, 'Oh, really?'

He plowed on. "I told you my friend Byron and his family were scammed but it wasn't that simple. At least, not for me and not for Byron. Byron was in his third year of medical school. I was in my fourth. We'd been friends all through med school. When he and his family bought into the scheme they lost all their money. Their money, Byron's money, their house. All but a very small amount, enough for his parents to live on for a short while. But Byron had nothing. He not only had to drop out of school, but he lived with me until he found a full-time job and got back on his feet. His part-time job paid barely enough to buy peanut butter, much less rent an apartment.

"I had a lot of student debt. My dad was gone by then. Mom was struggling and there were three of us. Liam was just starting raising his horses. Connor was in paramedic training. If I'd had the money, I'd have lent it to Byron to finish school, but I didn't. Turns out it was a good thing because I hadn't had the money to invest in the scheme either. I don't think I would have anyway. It seemed off to me."

"I'm sorry about your friend and his family," Cici said finally. "I wish it hadn't happened. I wish my parents hadn't done it. But that doesn't explain why it was so easy for you to believe the worst of me. Or why you wouldn't even let me tell you what happened."

He'd fucked up badly. He should have told her about Janelle and Beth. Because they were the reason he'd reacted as he had as much or more than Byron. But he didn't believe anything he said would matter now.

"Will you tell me now?" he asked.

"When all this happened, I wasn't living at home. I'd been on my own, supporting myself, for a long time. The first I knew of it was when a friend of mine told me about this investment plan my parents were running. Fran hadn't bought into it because she was very suspicious. I could have blown it off. It was one person's opinion and they were my parents. But Fran is a very solid, careful person who wouldn't have mentioned it to me without good reason. So I investigated. And I found out it was true."

"Is that when you turned them in?"

"No. Not right then. I confronted them. I begged them to stop and return what money they could. Of course, they'd already spent a massive amount. They wouldn't stop. They even laughed at me. They didn't seem to realize or maybe they didn't care that what they were doing was wrong, even criminal. So I turned them in."

"That must have been hard."

"You have no idea. And just fyi, the SEC didn't automatically assume I was involved. The first thing they did was clear me."

Neither did I, he started to say but she was continuing, clearly uninterested in anything he had to say.

"Try to imagine turning in your parents for fraud. They went to prison. Because of me. My father forgave me, but my mother hasn't and never will. They are still my parents. I still love them. But what they were doing was wrong. So wrong."

"I'm sorry, Cici. It sounds horrible."

"It was. That's not even the worst part. I told you my father died. He was shanked in the prison showers. Where he wouldn't have been if not for me."

Nothing he said would make a difference, nevertheless he

said, "I'm so sorry."

"So am I. I regret having to turn them in, but I know I'd do it again. And that makes me feel even worse."

"I'm sorry," Logan repeated. "I was wrong. Can you forgive me?"

She stood and paced away a few steps before turning back to him. "It's not a matter of forgiving you. I can forgive you. I do forgive you. I can even understand why you were so angry, given the circumstances."

"Then...we're okay?"

She looked at him sadly. "No. I forgive you but I can't get past it."

"Ever?"

HOW WAS SHE supposed to get past something like this? She couldn't simply accept that the man she loved, the man she'd thought loved her, could believe her capable of committing fraud on a massive scale. "You asked me to marry you, Logan. To be your wife, presumably forever. And then, the minute you learned of it, you turned around and accused me of being a part of my parents' fraud."

"I didn't...accuse you."

"All but. Why do you think I left Fort Worth? Can you imagine what it was like for me? I couldn't stand being the subject of so much speculation. I heard the whispers. *She had to have known. She turned in her parents so she wouldn't get charged. Of course she made a deal.* And on and on. My real friends believed in me, but no one else did. Apparently, not even the man who asked me to marry him." When he said nothing she continued. "Liam believes me. He said anyone who knew me wouldn't believe I'd be a party to committing fraud. Guess he was wrong, huh?"

Logan looked sad and…defeated. She'd never seen him look that way. Hadn't known he *could* look that way. More than anything she wanted to comfort him, to tell him she forgave him and of course they could work it out. But that would be a lie so she didn't say it.

"So this is the end," he said, anger roughening his voice. "You want to throw away what we have—what we could have—because I screwed up. You won't even give me a chance to make it up to you."

"That's not it. I can see that you're sorry. But what kind of relationship could we have when you're capable of believing I was involved in that fraudulent scheme? A Ponzi scheme that cost some people their life savings. What's to say you wouldn't do the same thing again in another situation?" She shook her head. "I can't live like that, Logan."

He got up. "You say you can forgive me but it's damn clear you haven't. I still love you, Cici. And beneath all the hurt and anger, I think you still love me. If you change your mind and realize this is something we should be able to work through, give me a call."

He walked out the door. She went to the door and locked it. She turned around, her back to the door, and slid down to the floor. She pulled up her knees, put her arms around them, buried her head and cried.

Chapter Twenty-Three

"My God, Logan," Connor said when Logan opened his apartment door a few days later. "You look like shit. What happened?"

Liam walked up in time to hear Connor's question. "He fucked up, that's what happened," Liam said.

Trust Liam to get straight to the point.

They both entered and sat on Logan's couch. "Why are we here?" Connor asked him.

"Want a beer?" Liam asked, going to the kitchen and opening the refrigerator door.

Both Connor and Logan said yes. Liam brought each one a can and then sat back down. "She won't take you back, huh?" Liam asked.

"No." He didn't really think either of his brothers could help him but hell, what were brothers for if not to commiserate when you fucked up? Not that Liam looked particularly sympathetic.

"You and Cici broke up?" Connor asked. "I thought you were really crazy about her."

"I was. I am. But she says we're done."

"Tell him why," Liam said.

Logan glared at Liam. "I haven't told you why."

"I can guess."

Logan contemplated slugging him, but it was too much trouble.

Looking from one to the other Connor said, "Someone clue me in because I don't have a flipping clue what's going on."

So he told him, including that she'd said she had no part in the scam and he...well, he'd been skeptical. Finishing up, he said, "Now she says she forgives me, but she can't get past it. So we're done."

"What's wrong with you?" Connor asked. "I hardly know her and I wouldn't have believed Cici would do that. Why in the hell did you?"

"I didn't. I don't." He rubbed a hand over his forehead. "I didn't want to but when Byron told me and she hadn't mentioned a word about it—Hell, I didn't even know her real name." He shrugged. "Anyway, I finally got her to at least let me explain. I told her about Byron in more detail and that's when she said she'd forgive me. But she won't give me another chance. She says we can't have a relationship if that's what I think of her. And it doesn't seem to matter to her that I don't think she could be capable of fraud. It was a momentary lapse."

"Do you blame her?" Liam asked.

"No. But I want her. I'm in love with her. Before this

happened, I asked her to marry me but she wouldn't give me an answer. I guess I know why now."

Both his brothers were looking at him like he was crazy. "You asked her to marry you?" Connor asked. "That was quick."

"When you know, you know."

"Let me get this straight," Connor said. "You asked her to marry you and then you immediately decided she was part of a Ponzi scheme?"

When he said it like that it made him feel even dumber than he already did.

"Did you tell her about Beth?" Liam asked.

"No."

"Why not? You know that's probably the major reason why you believed Cici might be involved."

"I don't think Cici is like Beth. I never have."

"Maybe not," Connor said. "But you don't trust yourself. You don't trust your judgment. If you did you wouldn't have screwed up so badly."

"Gee, thanks, Connor. I never thought of that."

Connor laughed. "If you want my advice—"

"I don't."

"Then why the hell did you ask us over here?"

Liam interrupted before they could really get into it. "She's still in love with you. Give her some time. And then tell her about Beth."

"I'll think about it."

They both left shortly after that, leaving Logan to stew. It irritated the hell out of him whenever he realized one of his brothers was right. It was usually Liam, but this time it was both of them. But while Connor acted and usually was easygoing, he also had a very sharp mind and a strong work ethic and he could be surprisingly perceptive. Not that it took a lot of insight to realize Logan had totally screwed up. He'd kept his mouth shut after Liam had told him to give Cici time, happy they both left soon after.

Liam's comments had Logan asking himself why he was conceding defeat when he still loved Cici and she still loved him. Because he did not believe she'd fallen out of love with him so quickly. And if she could forgive him, which she said she had, then there was bound to be a way to convince her to give him another chance.

Fine. He'd give her time. No matter how badly he wanted to see her, he was backing off. For now. But damn sure not forever.

IT HAD ONLY been a few days since Logan had come to Cici's apartment and she'd told him they were done. But it had been forever since she'd made love with him or even kissed him. Damn, she missed him so much it was a physical ache. She'd seen him several times. Glimpses of him at the hospital or around town. She wondered how long it would be before she could see him and not want him desperately.

It wasn't just the sex, either. Although she sure as hell missed that. But she missed talking to him, whether it was a short conversation about ordinary things or a long involved discussion of a subject they were both passionate about. She missed simply being with him while she worked on her book and he read one of his medical journals. She missed going out with him for dinner or somewhere fun. It had been years since she'd bowled or played miniature golf, but she'd done both with Logan and thoroughly enjoyed herself.

In fact, she missed every damn thing about him and the two of them together.

Her computer was open with the cursor blinking on a blank page. Damn it, how was she supposed to work on her book when her mind was full of Logan?

Cici heard the knock on her door and thankfully got up to answer it. When she opened the door her friend Letty stood there.

"Letty, what's up?" She opened the door wider so Letty could come in.

"Did you forget we had a lunch date?" Letty said as she walked inside.

"Oh, crap. That was today?"

"You said you were going to put it in your phone."

"I did but I haven't looked at my phone in two days. I'm pretty sure it's dead." Not that it had helped her write.

Letty tossed her purse onto a chair and sat on the couch.

Looking around, she said, "I take it this book is kicking your ass."

"In a word, yes." Cici wore her oldest, rattiest sweatpants and shirt. Her hair needed washing but instead she'd pulled it back and stuck it on top of her head with a banana clip.

Letty crossed her legs and leaned back. "Maybe the problem isn't the book. Maybe it's you and Logan."

"There is no me and Logan. Not anymore. You know that."

"Are you sure that's what you want? Do you still love him?"

"Yes, and I wish to hell I didn't."

"How long has it been since you've seen him?"

"A few days." But it felt like forever.

"Do you miss him?"

"Only more than I thought it was possible to miss someone. Like I'm missing a part of myself. But we weren't even together that long. How could I miss him so much?"

"The question is if you miss him and love him then why the hell aren't you with him?"

"I told you why. If he thinks so little of me, how can we be together?"

"Oh, give it a rest, Cici."

Cici just goggled at her.

Her friend continued. "Logan made a mistake. Was it stupid? Absolutely. But he apologized and wanted to make things right and you cut him off at the knees."

"I wouldn't go that far."

"I would. You're punishing him for one mistake. It was a big mistake, but still only one mistake. And you're punishing yourself as much as you are him."

"You're supposed to be my friend. Why are you sticking up for Logan?"

"Because you belong together and I'm tired of seeing you miserable."

Letty had a point. Especially about her being miserable. Did she and Logan belong together? That she didn't know.

"How long are you going to make him wait?"

"I don't know. I thought we were done."

"Even though you don't want that any more than he does."

"I don't know, Letty. I do know I have three days to finish this book. That's my priority right now. After I turn it in I'll decide what to do." Of course, what to do depended on Logan and how he felt. Maybe he was glad they were done. Glad that he'd escaped. Happy she hadn't answered when he asked her to marry him.

If that's how he felt, she deserved it.

IT HAD BEEN three weeks and two days since he and Cici had broken up. Logan wasn't sure if that was long enough for her, but it was plenty long enough for him. He wasn't giving up. He knew she'd had a book deadline, but he had not-so-subtly asked Letty about it and she'd told him the due date.

"It was today, but you should give her a couple of days to sleep," Letty had said. "If I know her, she's pulled several all-nighters to get the book done."

So, he waited for a couple of days and said to hell with it. He'd waited long enough. He went to her apartment, climbed the stairs and rang her doorbell. She opened the door and his first good look at her hit him like a sledgehammer.

Her hair was loose, falling in rich brown waves past her shoulders. Her big, brown eyes widened with surprise. She wasn't dressed up, per se, but she wore fitted jeans that showed off beautiful curves, and a fitted soft blue sweater. She wore makeup that accented her eyes and lipstick—red, naturally—that she didn't often wear.

Oh, shit. She was going out.

"Hi. Sorry, did I catch you at a bad time?"

"No. I have a little while before I need to leave. What do you need?"

You, he wanted to say. *Please don't tell me you have a date*, he thought, although he suspected she did. And why shouldn't she? He had no claim on her. Not anymore.

When he said nothing but stood in the open doorway, she opened the door wider. "Well, come in. It's cold and we're letting out the warm air."

He did as she said, and draped his jacket over a chair, not

really knowing how to begin. Finally he decided to simply be honest. "I've been thinking a lot about the two of us. About how badly I fucked up and was there any way I could fix it."

"And what did you decide?"

"I love you and I want us to be together. I will do anything I have to, to put us back together. I'm not giving up until I find a way. Because not only do I love you but I think you still love me."

She stared at him.

"I know the problem is that you can't get past me thinking you could have been involved with your parents' scam. But I didn't really think it was possible. The doubts I had weren't because I didn't trust you. I didn't trust my own judgement. And the reason for that lies in my past, which we've never talked about." He drew in a breath and asked, "Can I tell you about it?"

Chapter Twenty-Four

HE WANTED TO open up to her.

If she let him explain, tell her about his past, she wouldn't be able to maintain the distance between them. She'd already forgiven him but could she ever get past what he'd done? More importantly, what he'd thought of her?

Cici didn't know but she had no choice but to listen. "I'm listening." She sat on the couch. Logan started to pace.

"During my residency I was involved with a woman, a woman I wanted to marry, though not until I got out of residency. Beth was a resident too so it made no sense for us to plan anything until we were both finished. But we were serious." He fell silent.

"Were you in love with her?"

"Oh, yeah. Big time. She was smart, beautiful, driven—everything I thought I wanted in a woman. I was…dazzled. And apparently, naive as hell."

"You don't strike me as naive."

"Not now, but I was then." He passed a hand over his eyes, then let both hands fall to his thighs, tightening into fists. "We were both in surgery, but she was a year behind me. I was the chief resident and Beth was determined to be chief resident her last year, but her competition was stiff. She made a mistake during one of her rotations. The patient lived but it was touch and go. So to cover her mistake she falsified data on the patient. One of her colleagues turned her in but she got out of it. I believed her. I believed everything she told me. None of it was true.

"The second time she made a bad mistake, the patient died. She tried to cover it up again by framing another resident but that didn't work. She wound up getting kicked out of the program." He shook his head and continued. "Doctors make mistakes. Sometimes people die. It wasn't so much that she'd screwed up, but the attempted cover-up and framing another resident was something that couldn't be overlooked. Couldn't be tolerated."

"Did you believe her that time?"

"Yes. I had to have her guilt proved to me before I believed she'd actually done what she was accused of. God, I felt like a fool. I didn't see through her. I bought into every lie. I wouldn't listen to anyone who had tried to warn me she wasn't what she seemed."

"What happened then?"

"Once I finally figured out her true character, I broke it off with her. And I haven't been serious about anyone since. Until I met you."

"You thought I was a liar, like her."

"I didn't believe you were involved with the scam. I

couldn't imagine you doing something like that. But…I didn't trust myself, which was why I reacted the way I did. By the time I realized what a fool I'd been it was too late. You were done with me."

"I don't know what to say, Logan."

He stopped pacing and looked at her with his heart in his eyes. "Say you'll give me another chance. I love you so much, Cici. I don't want to live without you."

She'd said she'd forgiven him, but had she really? Saying she couldn't get past what he had thought of her wasn't forgiving. It was holding a grudge. Was she going to let what she and Logan had together go, simply because she couldn't forgive him a mistake? A mistake he'd owned? She'd made mistakes too. She should have told Logan about her parents long before this. She should have told him the moment she realized she loved him. But she'd waited and he'd learned about it in the worst way.

"I've missed you, Logan. More than I thought possible. I thought I'd get used to being without you but I haven't. It's only gotten worse."

"What are you saying?"

"I'm saying you weren't the only one who was a fool. If I'd told you about my family when we first grew closer, this wouldn't have happened." She rose and walked over to him. "I thought I could get over you but if the last few weeks are any example, that's not going to happen. I love you too, Logan."

"Thank God," he said and pulled her into his arms.

His mouth came down on hers. Straining, she rose on her toes and kissed him back, tongues tangling, bodies pressed together. He boosted her up, she wrapped her legs around him, peppering kisses all over his face as he walked them to her bed. He set her down and they both started stripping, flinging clothes everywhere.

They came together, falling on the bed, rolling over it with Cici on top first, then Logan. "Hurry," Cici said.

But instead of hurrying he slowed down, tasting her nipples, running his hands over her body in long, slow strokes. "I've missed you so much. Missed everything about you." His voice was muffled since he was placing kisses on her bare skin as he spoke.

"I missed you too. And I want you inside me now."

He smiled and then paused. "I don't have a condom. I wasn't expecting this."

"What were you expecting?"

"You to kick me out."

"Oh, Logan. I'm so sorry."

"Why? You have nothing to apologize for."

"Yes, I do. But we can argue about that later. Look in my bedside table drawer."

He did so, pulled one out and she snatched it from him. She ripped open the packet and rolled it down on him. She wasn't having any slow going. The moment she got the condom on she positioned herself over him and took him inside her in one push, sinking down on him before raising up and doing it again. He met her, thrusting up as she came down. Moments later she came, exploding into a thousand pieces, hearing Logan shouting her name as he found his satisfaction. Cici collapsed on his chest. Long moments later she rolled aside and he kissed her before going into the bathroom to clean up.

When he returned he pulled her into his arms and kissed her forehead. She laughed and snuggled against him. She hadn't felt this content…ever.

LOGAN HAD NEVER been much of a cuddler. Except with Cici it felt right. When she returned from the bathroom she lay down beside him and snuggled against him, one arm across his waist and her head on his chest. Lying in bed naked with Cici, stroking that soft, soft skin, thinking about how soon he could—

"Oh, no!" Cici had been tracing something on his chest with her fingers but at the exclamation she sat up in bed clutching the sheet to her breasts.

"What's wrong?"

"I forgot I was supposed to meet some friends at the Graff for drinks." She grabbed her phone and checked the time. "An hour ago. Great, there are seven messages. I had the phone silenced."

"Aren't you going to read them?"

She typed something into her phone before putting it down. "No need. I know what they say."

"You had a date?" Damn, he'd worried about that when he first saw her.

"Yes. With the girls." She smiled. "You were afraid it was with a man."

"Damn right I was."

She leaned over and kissed him. "I'm hung up on you. I have no desire to go out with another man."

"Good." He kissed her again. "So we're okay now, right?"

"I think we're a little better than okay."

"Are we? I think I should check." He tumbled her onto her back and began stringing kisses down her body.

"Logan, we should…"

He looked up and smiled at her. "We should what?"

"Nothing. Don't stop."

"Don't worry, I won't."

When they finally got out of bed Logan decided there was something he wanted to do. Something he should probably wait on but he was just so damn happy to be with Cici again he didn't think he could wait.

"Let's go for a ride."

"Horseback or car?"

"Horseback. I need to stop by my apartment and change on the way to the ranch." He needed to put on his jeans and boots, so Cici wouldn't question why he wanted to go to his apartment. But he doubted she would have any idea of his real reason for stopping there.

"Okay."

It didn't take Logan long to get dressed. While he waited for Cici he tried to tell himself not to be in such a hurry. Although he and Cici were back together that didn't mean she was ready to really commit to him. He should wait. Give her more time.

Yeah. That wasn't happening.

Chapter Twenty-Five

THEY DIDN'T SEE anyone when they got to the ranch. Liam was off somewhere, almost certainly with one or more of the horses. Maureen's car wasn't there, which made Cici feel guilty because she was relieved. They didn't go in the main house so they didn't see Velma. Other than the dogs milling around and Rambler being ecstatic to see Logan, it was a quiet day at the ranch.

Cici rode Angus, the mild-mannered horse she'd ridden since she came to Montana. Logan had asked her if she wanted a different horse but she said no. She liked the big roan gelding and felt comfortable with him by now. She'd told Liam she didn't need a horse who would 'go faster,' thank you. She liked slow just fine. Logan rode a gorgeous black mare named Annie he said was the one he usually rode unless one of the others needed exercising. But since Liam wasn't around to say, he rode Annie.

They took the path that led to the creek. One she was familiar with since Liam had taken her on it several times. She wondered what had made Logan suddenly decide they needed to go riding. Not that she minded, she just thought it was a little odd.

They stopped by the stream, farther down than where she'd sat with Liam when she'd first arrived. "I love this creek," Logan said. "My brothers and I used to play here when we were kids. We'd ride the horses down here, usually bareback, and shove each other in the water when it was hot. A few times when it was cold, too." He grinned at that.

"Sounds like fun."

"It was. This has always been a special place for me. Which is why I brought you out here."

She waited, wondering where he was going with this. He'd been standing beside the creek holding her hand, but he let go and got down on one knee. Her heart started pounding. She hadn't expected this, certainly not now. They'd just gotten back together.

He pulled something out of his pocket and held it out to her. It was a beautiful diamond solitaire surrounded by smaller diamonds. "Cici, I love you so much. Being without you made me realize that I didn't want to be without you. Ever. You mean everything to me."

Before she could say anything he continued. "I know I should have waited but I've wanted to marry you almost since the day I met you. Unfortunately, you had that pesky relationship with my brother. So I didn't really think about it until we got together. And then you said no—"

"I said not yet. And not to bring up sore subjects but I wanted to tell you about my family before I answered you."

"And then I was a dumbass and then you forgave me, and I couldn't wait any longer. I love you, Cici. Will you marry me?"

She sank to her knees too. "Oh, Logan. I love you too. Yes, I'll marry you." She held out her left hand.

He put the ring on her finger and kissed her hand and then she was in his arms kissing him. When they finally drew apart—mostly because the rocky ground by the creek was killing her knees—Logan helped her rise.

"I want us to get married soon," he said.

"Okay. How soon?"

"Tomorrow?"

She laughed. "Seriously."

"I am serious. But we can wait a couple of weeks if we have to."

"We won't be able to get a church that fast."

"We'll get married here at the ranch. Mom and Velma will love it."

"I think you should talk to your mother before deciding. She may object to you marrying me."

"She won't. Do you mind if we keep it small? Family and close friends?"

"Of course not."

She didn't think her expression betrayed anything but Logan said, "You're thinking about your parents, aren't you?"

"Yes," she said, seeing no reason to lie when he knew she

was. "My mother wouldn't come anyway, even if she wasn't in prison. I'm pretty sure she'll never forgive me." And her father was dead. She'd always imagined that her dad would give her away when she got married. But if she thought any more about her father she'd cry and there wasn't a thing she could do about it. She shook her head, not wanting to ruin this moment.

"We can work on the list but Roxanne, Letty, and a couple of the women I've met since I got here are the only people I definitely want to come. I'm sure Roxanne can arrange to come up for a few days."

"Great. Let's go tell my family and we can get started planning."

"Logan, are you sure we shouldn't wait a while? We did just get back together."

He took both her hands and carried them to his lips. "I'm sure but if you're not ready just tell me. I don't want to rush you if you're not sure."

"I'm sure I want to marry you whenever you want."

"Good answer," he said, and kissed her.

THEY SET THE date for late October. Logan's wedding day dawned bright and beautiful. There was a chill in the air but it was crisp rather than cold. Both of his brothers were standing up for him. Connor was able to take a couple of days off and Liam had even arranged for his new hand to take care of the animals for the day and evening of the wedding. As for Logan himself, he'd managed to get a week off with a combination of bribery and calling in favors so he'd be covered at the hospital while he got married and went on a short honeymoon.

Last night the wedding party, which included almost all the invited guests, had gone to Rosita's Mexican Grill for the rehearsal dinner. It had been casual and fun with several people imbibing a little too freely of the margaritas. Both Logan and Cici were careful because neither wanted to be hungover on their wedding day.

Velma had begun cooking for the reception almost from the day they told everyone. They'd offered to see if they could find someone to cater it but Velma had vehemently vetoed that idea. Logan was her first 'boy' getting married and she intended to help give them a wedding they'd all remember.

If his mom had doubts, she kept them to herself. To his relief, Maureen had welcomed Cici into the family and according to Cici she'd been very sweet to her. Now if only they could convince Maureen that Liam was okay. He'd found a ranch manager he believed would work out, and hired another full-time hand, plus a couple more part-timers, but who knew if Maureen would buy off on that?

Finally, it was time for the ceremony. Logan waited for Cici, Liam and Connor at his side. Letty came first, then

Roxanne, the maid of honor, followed. The music changed and he saw Cici. She literally took his breath away. She'd left her hair down and it curled around her shoulders and down her back in rich brown waves. She'd done something to make her eyes look larger and more mysterious. When she saw him she smiled, the smile that seemed just for him. Her white wedding dress was a strapless, low-cut gown, fitted at the waist and top, and flowing gently to the floor. She was gorgeous.

The ceremony was traditional, with traditional vows, for which he was extremely grateful because the idea of writing his own vows made him break out in a cold sweat. Besides, it was all he could do to concentrate on repeating the well-known words when Cici stood in front of him looking more beautiful than he'd ever seen her.

"I now pronounce you husband and wife. You may now kiss the bride," the preacher intoned.

Logan took her in his arms and kissed her, not letting up until his brothers pulled Cici out of his arms to kiss her themselves.

"Okay, that's it," he told them, drawing Cici back to himself. "That's the last time either of you gets to put your lips on my wife."

Cici laughed along with them. "You're the only one I want," she told Logan. So of course, he had to kiss her again.

THE WRONG BROTHER

EVERYONE PRESENT HAD been invited to both the wedding and the reception. It was a little larger than they'd wanted but that couldn't be helped. Their close friends were there, including some of the doctors Logan worked with and some of the other friends Cici had made since coming to Montana. Clint and his family were there, as were the Fletchers—Liam's best friend Riley and his younger sister Val, and both his parents. Cici was happy Val was no longer shooting her death glares, but she'd stopped that weeks ago when she'd found out that Cici was with Logan rather than Liam.

"Having fun?" Logan asked Cici.

"It's wonderful. The wedding was perfect. Now I just need food before I faint. I was too nervous to eat before."

Logan kissed her and left to get her a plate of food. She had a moment to herself and saw Liam and Val in what looked like an intense discussion before she waved him away and left the room. Liam stood looking after her with a puzzled expression. When Logan returned with her food, she thanked him and ate a bit before speaking.

"Is something going on between Liam and Val?"

"Not that I know of. Why?"

"It looked like they were having some kind of deep discussion and then she left abruptly."

"No telling. They've known each other forever."

"I know, but does Liam realize Val's had a crush on him for years?"

"She has?"

"Of course she has. Anyone with eyes can see it."

"Liam doesn't," he said decisively.

She rolled her eyes. "I rest my case. Val looks very pretty tonight. I've never seen her in anything besides jeans."

"I wouldn't know. I haven't had eyes for anyone but my beautiful wife."

Cici sighed happily. "That was so sweet."

"Not sweet. Truthful." He picked up a canapé and fed it to her. "How soon can we leave?"

"Not for a while yet. Why are you in such a hurry?"

He leaned forward and spoke in her ear. "Because I can't wait to get you alone and naked. I've been imagining getting you out of that dress since I saw you."

A thrill shot up her spine. "I want that too."

"Time to throw the bouquet," Letty said, some time later.

The single women gathered together, laughing and talking. Cici turned her back to them and said, "Ready?" She tossed the bouquet over her shoulder.

When she turned around she saw that all of them were looking at Val holding the flowers. Val looked bewildered. Cici hadn't seen her in the original group. She must have just walked into the room. Val stared at the bouquet for a moment, then shoved it at Letty and ran out of the room.

Whoa. Wonder why she did that?

"What are you staring at?" Logan asked her.

She shifted her gaze to her new husband. "Tell you later.

Right now I need you to spirit me away."

"Nothing would make me happier. At least until I get you alone."

"Promises, promises."

"Don't worry, I keep my promises," Logan said. And he kissed her.

The End

If you loved *The Wrong Brother*, keep an eye out for book two in the *Montana Made* series, featuring rancher **Liam McFarland** and his best friend's little sister, **Val Fletcher**.

It's called *The Christmas Cowboy*, and here's a taste!

She was some distance away, but he'd recognize Val Fletcher anywhere. Not only was she his best friend Riley's younger sister, but she was the one person around here who he wouldn't mind dating. If she hadn't been eight years younger than him in addition to being off limits because of his friendship with Riley.

But damn, she was a pretty girl. No, she'd turned into a beautiful woman. But five would get you ten that Riley didn't think of his little sis as a woman. Liam had talked to her earlier during the reception, before the bouquet incident. She'd looked upset and he'd asked her if something was wrong, but she'd denied it. However, the fact that she was double timing it to the barn wearing a short sleeved dress without even a sweater put lie to that comment. November was pretty cold in Marietta.

She wore a red dress with small white flowers that dipped low in the front, fit at the waist and then flared out. And when she walked the dress split and showed her long legs. Legs he'd noticed before, even when he knew he shouldn't. Yeah, he'd noticed the dress when he was talking to her earlier. So sue him. Unlike his friend, Liam had no problem believing Val was all grown up. Even if she was too young for him.

He walked in the barn and found her sitting on a hay bale, crying. Not just crying, but full-out sobbing as if her heart was broken. "Val? What's wrong?"

She looked up and, seeing him, began to wipe at her eyes with her fingers. "Oh, Liam. Nothing's wrong."

He sat beside her. "Obviously, something is. Otherwise, you wouldn't be out here without even a sweater crying like you just lost your best friend." He took off his jacket and laid it over her shoulders. "Come on, you can tell me. Maybe I can help."

"No, you can't. No one can."

He got up, went to the tack room, and came back with a box of tissues. "Here. Now, tell me what's going on."

She wiped her eyes, blew her nose, and took in a shaky breath. "I'm pregnant."

His eyes widened. "Pregnant?"

If you enjoyed *The Wrong Brother*,
you'll love the other books in…

Montana Made series

Book 1: *The Wrong Brother*

Book 2: *The Christmas Cowboy*

Available now at your favorite online retailer!

More books by Eve Gaddy

Texas True series
Book 1: *Texas Forged*
Book 2: *Truly, Madly Texas*
Book 3: *Texas Made*
Book 4: *Texas Cowgirl*
Book 5: *Hot Texas Trouble*
Book 6: *Texas Christmas Baby Bargain*

The Heart of Texas series
Book 1: *Heart of the Texas Doctor*
Book 2: *Texas on My Mind*
Book 3: *Under the Mistletoe*
Book 4: *Heart of the Texas Warrior*

The Devil's Rock at Whiskey River series
Book 1: *Rebel Pilot Texas Doctor*

Book 2: *His Best Friend's Sister*

Book 3: *No Ordinary Texas Billionaire*

The Gallaghers of Montana series

Book 1: *Sing Me Back Home*

Book 2: *Love Me, Cowgirl*

Book 3: *The Doctor's Christmas Proposal*

Book 4: *The Cowboy and the Doctor*

Book 5: *Return of the Cowgirl*

Available now at your favorite online retailer!

About the Author

Eve Gaddy is the award winning, national bestselling author of forty novels. Her books have sold over a million copies and been published in many countries and several languages. She writes contemporary romance, romantic suspense, romantic mystery, and a bit of paranormal romance as well.

Eve's books have won and been nominated for awards from Romantic Times, Golden Quill, Bookseller's Best, Holt Medallion, Daphne Du Maurier and many more. Eve was awarded the 2008 Romantic Times Career Achievement award for Series Storyteller of the year, and was nominated for a Romantic Times Career Achievement Award for Innovative Series romance. She loves her family, books, electronics, the mountains, and East Texas in the spring and fall. She also loves a happy ending. That's why she writes romance.

Thank you for reading

The Wrong Brother

If you enjoyed this book, you can find more from all our great authors at TulePublishing.com, or from your favorite online retailer.

Made in United States
Troutdale, OR
10/14/2024